Thank you for
reading,, Vickie!
Enjoy!

God Bless,

[signature]

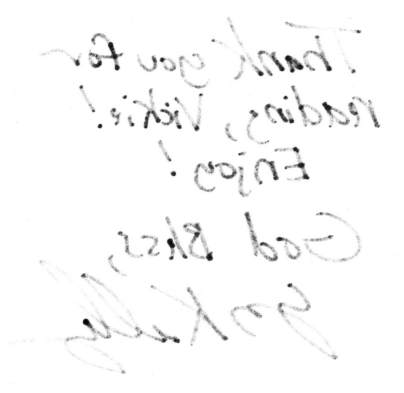

Thank you for reading, Vickie! Enjoy!

God Bless,

DARK LANDS
REQUIEM

Lyn I. Kelly

ISBN: 978-1-4834-3423-0 (sc)
ISBN: 978-1-4834-3422-3 (e)

Because of the dynamic nature of the Internet, any web addresses or links contained in this book may have changed since publication and may no longer be valid. The views expressed in this work are solely those of the author and do not necessarily reflect the views of the publisher, and the publisher hereby disclaims any responsibility for them.

Any people depicted in stock imagery provided by Thinkstock are models, and such images are being used for illustrative purposes only.
Certain stock imagery © Thinkstock.

Black Kitty Productions Logo courtesy of Mike Murdock. No reproduction of this work without the authorized consent of the artist.

Lulu Publishing Services rev. date: 08/26/2015

ACKNOWLEDGEMENTS

The first person I want to thank is my wife, Hera. You are my Love, my confidant, my best friend, my soul mate. You are the woman who made me feel good about myself again, who allowed me to accept the real me. Thank you for giving me the courage and confidence to get *Dark Lands* published. I Love You so very much. I want to thank my mother, she who openly encouraged my imagination when so many others discouraged it. She is the one who fought and sacrificed. I Love You, mom. I thank you for everything. My successes are yours. My failures are my own. I want to thank my children, Kalyn and Seth, for enthusiastically reading my manuscript and giving me ideas when I was "stuck". I Love You both. You have helped me more than you know. I want to thank my brother, Owen, for your support. I Love You. You may be my younger brother, but I look up to you more than you could ever possibly appreciate. I want to thank my Dad for giving me my love of reading and jogging, both of which keep me sane. I Love You, dad. Thank you for being there. I want to thank Mike Murdock, the greatest artist I have ever known and the best friend anyone could ever have. You have selflessly been there regardless of the situation. I want to thank Tommy Thompson. You are a good man and I Love You very much. Thank you for all you have done and continue to do. I want to thank Logan and Lacey for accepting me into their lives and giving me the benefit of the doubt. I Love You both. I want to thank, Meme. I know you are looking from above on all of us and forever watching. Thank you for always providing me a way when I thought there was not one. I Love You. This list would not be complete without thanking Mandy, Katie Grace, Hank, Susie, Carol, Ron, Kalee, Brent, Greg, Tommy and Lou. There are many others. You know who you are and you are all in my thoughts and prayers. Finally, I want to thank the Good Lord, Jesus the Christ, for Blessing me and never giving up on me.

Dedicated to
Mr. Tom Hays,
the teacher who taught me to truly appreciate the English language

"And with a word, it was all created—some worlds much different than others and not all of them known."
-The Willkeeper's Journal of Infinity: Infinity+1

CHAPTER ONE

GROWLERS

He lay crumpled on the ground, his body feeling as if it were distending, swelling in and out like waves crashing and receding against a shoreline. The sharp leaden smell of ozone was pervasive around him. His stomach felt twisted, indecisively in flux between slight nausea and full-blown retching. From somewhere deep inside, a singular feeling of panic began to bubble up until it was boiling, burning and tearing at him, until it tore him out of his catatonic state. And then Webb Thompson screamed.

"SUNDOWN!" The name roared out with such force that he could scarcely recognize his own voice. The escape of the desperate cry rubbed his throat raw, almost making him wonder whether he had shouted voluntarily or if the wild sound had released itself. His eyes followed the eerie repetitions of his echo as it bounced around the unfamiliar landscape.

Where was he?

Swallowing hard to relieve the increasing apprehension welling up from his chest, he began to shout once for her again, but this time, the words caught in his throat. There in the distance lay a young girl.

Webb languidly rose from his knees and slogged towards her, fighting the fear of what he might find when he got there. Stumbling to a halt beside her, he cradled his little sister in his arms. She was still breathing and blessedly alive.

"Sundown," he beckoned. He brushed the strands of wavy brown hair away from her face and rubbed her cold cheek, trying to wake her up.

Her eyes gradually flickered open and attempted to focus on his. Immediately, her expression registered the same confusion and sickness that Webb was feeling.

"Webb… Where are we?" she coughed weakly. "I feel sick…"

After gently moving her to a sitting position and making sure she was okay, Webb was finally calm enough to take in their surroundings. As far as the horizon stretched, he saw never-ending rolling hills and plains of grass, the richest, most perfect Webb had ever seen. The color was strangely vibrant, almost glowing. He grazed his hand across the grassy plain they sat upon, expecting to find the usual prickly coarseness, but instead discovering that the green blades had a soft silky texture on par with the finest of Egyptian cottons.

A sharp rumble jerked his attention upward. The sky was roiling in varying degrees of gray and somber black, as if the most violent of all thunderstorms was hiding just behind the cloud cover. But for all of the fury raging in the skies above them, the air immediately around Webb and Sundown was quiet and still. Too still.

"…Webb?" repeated Sundown. She sounded frightened.

"I don't know where we are, Sundown," he choked reluctantly. "I'm sorry. I don't even know how we got here…"

Fear was starting to creep over him like the skin of ice across a winter pond. It chilled his bones and goose bumps spread across his arms, but he kept his voice steady. In all his seventeen years, he had never seen a place as vividly haunting as this. Making the situation even more surreal was the fact that his memories were incomplete; they felt confused and jagged like a jumbled up jigsaw puzzle. *How had they gotten here?* With no memories to rationalize their current circumstances, even the panic that had so violently awoken him now seemed to have no meaning behind it. Their surroundings were as beautiful as they were unnerving, but the situation as a whole was nothing but terrifying.

He stood and helped Sundown to her feet, brushing the dirt and grass from her clothes. "Let's move, Sunny. There's bound to be someone around here who can help us," he said.

His voice was masked in a very confident, very forced bravado. He didn't know where they were going, but there was no sense in just standing around, waiting for help that might never come. They needed to make their own way. Choosing a direction to travel, however, would be difficult. They were in the midst of a vast verdant nothingness that stretched on in every direction. There were no evident landmarks to aim for and with the sky covered in clouds, he didn't even have the sun as a compass point to guide him. The only obvious distinction he could make out was that the sky rumbling behind them appeared much angrier and turbulent than the skies before them. They would be going that way, then.

"Where are Mom and Dad, Webb?" Sundown abruptly asked, interrupting his thoughts. Her voice heightened fearfully. "Where are they, Webb? Where *are* they!?"

"I don't know!" Webb replied sharply. He was tired and scared too, so his tone had been more abrasive than he'd intended. He spoke again, softly. "I don't know. But we're not going to find them by waiting here."

He gave his sister a reassuring hug and took a few steps forward to lead, but stopped when he sensed that Sundown hadn't followed. He turned around. Inexplicably, she had gone ghostly white, her gaze glassy and lethargic. "Sunny?" he called cautiously.

"...*Webb*," came the hollow reply, her voice cold and vacuous.

Alarmed, he moved towards her only to watch as her color suddenly returned. For a moment, she remained quiet, her eyes darting back and forth, as if she had just awoken from a dream. Then, she found her voice.

"I'm... I'm not a baby," she began hesitantly at first, but raised her voice with each successive statement. "And... and you will not boss me around like one. I am fourteen years old! If I want to stay here, I will stay here!" She pursed her lips and adamantly crossed her arms in punctuation.

Webb blinked in confusion. *Had he missed something?* "What are you talking about?" he asked exasperatedly, but before he could say anything more, a new sound emerged from behind them and broke the awkward standoff.

It wasn't very noticeable at first—a slight buzzing, not unlike that of a house fly. But then it began to transform into a louder, much more bodily reverberation. And it wasn't just one little sound, but the droning ebb and flow of multiple sounds from various directions. Several… *things* were closing in on them. Webb looked around, but the horizon was still vacant. There was nothing to be seen. The eerie noise alone, however, was enough to tell him to get out of there.

He grabbed Sundown's arm. "Let's go!" This time she did not protest.

They ran quickly across the slick grass, hoping to find shelter, newfound terror sloughing off any remaining lethargy or nausea that had plagued the two only moments before. As hard and as far as they ran, the scenery before them didn't change: more green fields and black skies. The only difference lay in the unknown noises pursuing them; they were getting louder and closer. And whatever they were, they were no longer buzzing. Now they were *growling.*

Webb looked back over his shoulder as he fled, trying to catch a glimpse of what could be pursuing them, but this time the landscape appeared strangely distorted. He wiped at his eyes, thinking that his pouring sweat had blurred his vision, but the distortion remained. Something hazy on the horizon was obstructing his view—something that was moving directly towards them. Something that was growling.

He pulled harder on his sister's arm. She wasn't keeping up with him. There was no way Sundown could keep running like this; even he could hardly keep going.

He stopped and turned to Sundown. "Keep going!" he shouted between gasps. "I'll catch up!"

Sundown hesitated but for a moment, fearful eyes meeting his through her bedraggled mess of hair before continuing her dogged pace.

Webb shaded his eyes with his hand and squinted. Between heaving breaths, he was finally able to see what was chasing them. They were gelatinous forms—watery with a dull, milky-gray sheen about them. From this distance, it was impossible to determine their size, but they were loosely spherical and palpitating, pulsating larger and smaller at random intervals. There was something almost serene about the way they glazed over the pastoral landscape, like dewdrops rolling down a blade of grass. Had it not been for the terrifying guttural sounds they emitted, he might have stood and watched their mesmerizing movements.

He turned and sprinted to catch up with his sister, terror again renewed. The growling by now had taken on a shrieking quality accompanied by low unholy moaning.

"Come on!" Webb screamed as he ran up beside her and took her hand, "We've got to run faster!"

But run to where? There was nothing to hide them.

Webb made a reluctant glance back and saw that the creatures had already overtaken the area where he had stopped to watch their advance only moments before. It was then that the gut-wrenching futility of the moment hit him. There was no choice. He and Sundown couldn't possibly escape. Those things were just too fast. Yet through the fog of hopelessness, one piercing thought rung through Webb's mind: *maybe Sundown could still get away.*

Sundown felt her brother's hand leave hers and she turned to find Webb fixated on their monstrous pursuers, feet planted firmly and fists balled in defiance against a charging hoard of watery abominations at least twice his size. She started to scream when out of the corner of her eye, she spotted a blur of movement in the distance and spun wildly to see something black darting towards them at lightning speed. Sundown swung back around, intent on telling Webb about this new threat, but she never got the chance.

Webb quickly threw his arms out, creating a barrier between her and the creatures. "Sundown, keep going!" he cried over the monsters' harsh growls. They would reach him any second now. In desperation, he closed his eyes and charged towards the nearest creature and sprang upon it, fists flying.

For a moment, Webb felt as if he'd splashed into an ice-cold body of water, but then the sensation violently changed into that of searing pain, like his body and soul were being dissolved at the seams. He wanted to scream, but was afraid to open his mouth, for fear that the burning liquid would find its way inside him. Then, just as suddenly, the pain stopped, replaced by a dull ache that pierced its way into his bones.

Webb shook his head and looked up. His momentum had carried him straight through the creature and onto the ground, where he'd collapsed in a wet sticky heap. The sick smell of ammonia rose off of him and his skin was pink and inflamed. Struggling through the haze of pain, Webb crawled back to where Sundown stood trembling and placed himself in front of her, aware as he did so, that the rest of the creatures began to encircle them like a pack of wolves. He became cognizant of Sundown's quivering hand on his shoulder as she fell absently to her knees behind him. He cupped her hand in his and then looked up as the creatures began to eerily transform, stretching and molding themselves into something resembling humanoid apparitions or banshees.

Webb suddenly felt, more than saw, a burst of movement to his right and he turned defensively, expecting to be overtaken by one of the horrible monsters. He braced himself for the searing pain. Instead, his eyes fell upon the largest house cat he had ever seen.

The dark feline paid no heed to Webb or Sundown. Instead, the cat focused its attention on the gelatinous monsters, hissing viciously at them. Its shining black fur was raised and prickled in anger.

The creatures stopped advancing, their desire to reach Webb and Sundown seemingly dashed by the cat's warning cries. They began to pulse in what seemed indecision, losing their ghost-like forms and melting back into shapeless blobs. The cat inched forward with its claws extended, hissing its warning all the while. The creature nearest the cat exploded with an enraged shriek; its misshapen form opened its disgusting wet mouth to howl at the skies above—but the black cat didn't budge. Webb suddenly realized with amazement that it was protecting him and Sundown.

Then, just as quickly as it started, the creature stopped screeching and hastily fled and the others followed slimily in its wake. Webb watched their retreat until the creatures dissolved into the horizon and the last echoes of their growls fell silent.

He turned towards Sundown who was still crouched behind him, white-knuckled, her jaw set and eyes wide. "Are you okay, Sunny?"

She was soaked in a sweaty mixture of fear and exhaustion. She softly placed her other hand on Webb's shoulder and stood up shakily. Webb followed suit and reached to steady her, but before he could, she suddenly fell back to the ground, unconscious.

"Sundown?" Webb gasped. He dropped back to his knees and looked over the girl. Sundown's breaths were slow and her face was peaceful and composed. She seemed to be okay, just in shock. He glanced helplessly over at the cat who was watching quietly over them. It met Webb's gaze and winked.

Webb didn't know how to react, but he was too tired to really even think about it. He felt himself being drawn towards the soft, welcoming ground and he didn't resist as his knees buckled underneath him. His eyelids grew heavy. He thought he could hear a voice calling to him in the distance. Stranger still was the familiarity of the voice—a voice he knew, but hadn't heard in a long time. Webb became vaguely aware of a pair of strong hands clutching his shoulders before everything descended entirely into darkness.

CHAPTER TWO

UNCLE MIKE

Webb bolted up right in bed, breathing rapidly. He looked around and the panic subsided. He was in his room. Asleep in bed. Everything was as it should be. He sighed and drew his hands over his face and hair which were slick with nervous perspiration. *What a bizarre dream.*

Webb stretched and then slowly rolled out from under the covers, shaking the sleep and odd visions from his head. Once on his feet, he heard a low purring sound. He looked to the foot of his bed and there it was—*the large black cat.*

Webb gasped and stumbled backwards towards the door and fell out of his room onto the hard stone flooring. He let out a groan as pain shot through his elbows and knees. *Wait, stone?* He kicked the door to his room shut and then began to scoot away from it, head darting from side to side.

That had been his room, but this certainly wasn't his home. He was in the middle of some long medieval-looking hallway with vaulted ceilings towering at least four stories high, dimly lit by chandeliers. The stone masonry which had broken his fall covered not only the floors, but the walls and ceilings as well. Webb began to hyperventilate and the thick smell of dust, wood and iron filled his lungs.

"Calm yourself, Webb," came the familiar voice again.

"…Uncle Mike?" Webb exhaled in relief. Jumping to his feet, Webb turned to find a man standing cloaked in the shadows. "Where am I and what is that monster cat in my room?" he spat out before realizing what he was saying—or more importantly, who he was speaking to. Then the insanity of the situation spiraled through his brain and he began to feel an unwelcome chill, the hairs on the back of his neck rising. *"How-"*

"Steady, Webb," his uncle repeated as he limped into view. He was dressed in his faded old jeans and a light sweater, while a polished wooden cane helped to support his step. "We've a lot to talk about, the least of which is your friend, Gustafson."

With that, he took his finger and casually pointed it in Webb's direction. Webb heard a click emanate from behind him and turned to see the door to his room slip open, the enormous cat slinking out moments later.

"G-Gustafson?"

"The *monster cat*," replied his uncle, nodding in the cat's direction.

Webb swallowed, his eyes darting uncertainly between his uncle and the big animal.

Uncle Mike slowly put his hand on Webb's shoulder. "We could stand here and stare at each other all day, or we could go eat and talk all this over. And trust me, you need to eat."

Webb nodded guardedly, his eyes darting all around him.

Sensing his confusion, his uncle gently gestured towards the hallway. "Follow me, Webb," he said as he turned and began limping away.

The older man's stocky frame ambled slowly into the shadows, his cane tapping and echoing with each step. Webb watched him warily for a few seconds before giving up and following suit himself. A purring Gustafson trailed lazily behind him.

CHAPTER THREE

THE COMFORTING
ROOM

T he intoxicating aroma of cheeseburgers and french fries wafted out from behind the door they approached, making Webb appreciate how famished he really was. When his uncle opened the door to the room, Webb stepped forward in anticipation only to have his uncle's arm reach out to stop him.

"Don't get too caught up on the *how's* and *why's*, Webb," he cautioned. "For now, just try and accept what you see. You'll make sense of it later." He then moved his arm and let the boy pass.

Webb turned a quizzical eye towards his uncle, but the moment he stepped into the room, lured in by the promising scent of fast food, all of his confusion and apprehension evaporated. All that remained was a strange sense of familiarity, as if he had known this place all his life.

The chamber was oval in shape with wainscoted walls lined by dark acacia shelves that were stacked full of books, boxes of trinkets and other miscellany that Webb couldn't even begin to identify. On either side of him were tables, each the same dark acacia wood as the shelves. The one to his right was set up as a work desk and the other was jury

11

rigged to serve as a dinner table, upon which sat a huge porcelain plate spilling over with french fries and a large, juicy double-cheeseburger. Webb's stomach happily grumbled its approval.

Before he could satiate his hunger however, his attention was drawn to a chest-high pedestal set in the very center of the room. Atop the elegant frame was a small brightly glowing terrarium, in which an ashen gray picklock box was encased.

"Webb," called Mike, cutting his nephew's gaze short. "Eat."

Webb nodded and moved to the makeshift dinner table and pulled out one of four bountiful leather chairs and sat down, the plush leather comfortably absorbing his weight. He quickly pulled the mountainous plate of food towards him and took a huge bite out of the cheeseburger; the meat and cheese seemed to melt in his mouth. He quickly scarfed down two more bites before setting the burger down and plowing into the crispy french fries, their saltiness attacking his taste buds and making him suddenly very thirsty. He was about to ask for a drink when a new voice rang from around the corner.

"I suppose you would like a large Coke?" asked an older man. He strode up to Webb smoothly and confidently, a large crystal glass held firmly in his hand. The waistcoat and slacks he wore were perfectly starched and crisp with not a stray wrinkle in sight; similarly, his face, lined with age and framed by a closely cropped salt and pepper beard, was possessed of the finest, most elegant features.

Trailing him was a round, younger but larger man who was all smiles. In fact, he seemed to beam with the most genuine smile Webb had ever seen. He too held something in his hand: a smallish brown teddy bear.

The old gentleman set the fizzy glass down in front of Webb and then offered his hand. "My name is Mathias."

Webb shook the extended hand without leaving his seat, an impropriety which his mother would have readily chastised him for were she present.

"I see you obviously recognize your uncle," stated Mathias as he walked around the table and took the seat directly opposite Webb. "And the gentleman taking the seat beside me is Iggy," he continued.

The quiet young man smiled at Webb with bright eyes and nodded without uttering a word. Webb nodded back awkwardly.

"You have a lot of questions," said Mathias. His voice was a soothing one and somewhat reminiscent of sweet toffee clicking against the teeth. "Luckily, we have a lot of answers. To be fair, I shall let you decide where to begin."

Webb wasted no time. "My Uncle Mike is dead. He died a few years ago. So, who's this?" he asked, hooking a thumb in Mike's direction.

"Oh, that *is* your uncle," replied Mathias matter-of-factly.

"Then… he's *not* dead?" Webb hesitantly asked.

"No, he is dead—in the same way as we all are," replied Mathias.

"As we *all* are?" Webb responded incredulously.

"You always give them the floor, Mathias, and it always causes problems," Michael mumbled under his breath.

"Courtesy dictates that we let our guest take the path that he is most comfortable with first, Michael."

"Yeah, but now he's all befuddled. Look at him, Mathias," he replied, watching his nephew's eyes blink and wander around nervously.

"Well, everyone's explanation must start somewhere, even if it is difficult to comprehend at first," Mathias argued.

"Uh, why don't you just explain it the best way you can, Mathias?" Webb interrupted. True, the situation was strange and polarizing, but he actually felt much more comfortable than his body language suggested. Whether it was Mathias' grandfatherly voice or his kind wizened face, Webb did not know, but there was something about him that made Webb trust him unquestionably.

Mathias nodded. "Let's start at the beginning then. That's always best," he smiled, slowly rubbing his well-manicured beard. "Billions of years ago, the point we record as *infinity plus one second*, a grand explosion eviscerated the space that we now call the universe, creating worlds and seeding the elements necessary for the propagation of life. And since that point, there has always been the cycle of life and death. Or at least, that is what you have been taught, yes?"

"Yeah, I guess," Webb responded hesitantly.

"What if I were to tell you that there exists a realm between life and death, a place not yet recorded or referenced in any theological, mythological or historical archive?"

"…Okay," Webb replied as his mind tried to wrap itself around the concept. His focus was so intense that he didn't even notice Gustafson jump up on the table and begin licking his french fries.

"The place I am describing to you is *the Dark Lands*. And it is the place in which you now reside."

"The Dark Lands?"

"A realm created at time's inception, yet existing outside of time itself. Fascinating, yes?"

Webb deflated into his chair. Mathias' practiced speech was not offering any solace to the boy's addled mind. "I am *so* lost," he slurred, looking distractedly at his plate, which was now empty thanks to Gustafson. "Dead. Alive. I just want an answer," Webb mumbled half-heartedly. "I think I'm taking it all very well though, if I *am* really dead."

"It is the room—not that you do not have good composure in and of yourself," chuckled Mathias.

Webb glanced up from where he slouched. "What's special about this room?"

"Aside from being my room," Mathias began with a playful smile, "it has a very pacifying effect on those who enter here. That is why we have these little sessions here and not in the open with the others."

Webb's heart skipped a beat. "Others? There are *others*? How many?"

"Hundreds. You and Sundown are the latest additions to our family."

Sundown! Webb jumped up from the table. He had somehow forgotten about her until this very moment. *She was dead too?*

"Your sister is fine," reassured Mathias, signaling for Webb to sit back down. "You will see her very soon, but we must get through your counseling first."

Webb uneasily complied and sat back down restlessly.

"Now that you've had a moment to catch your breath, let's pick up from where we left off. I believe you were wondering about whether you were alive or dead."

"Well, putting two and two together-"

"Doesn't always equal four, Webb," interrupted Mathias. "In fact, in the Dark Lands you'll find that more often than not, it equals five, six or sometimes even seven."

"That doesn't help me at all. I'm still confused," surrendered Webb.

"Indeed you are, but I believe it will become much clearer to you momentarily. First, make no mistake. In your former world, the *living world*, you are most certainly dead. You had to physically die there in order to arrive here. That is the only path to the Dark Lands."

"So, I *did* die..." Webb responded nauseously.

"You died a physical death. Nothing more. The fact that we are sitting here conversing means that you are still very much alive, albeit in a different sense than you are used to. And that is very important."

Webb shook his head. "Well, that's great, but I need to get back to my parents. They must be worried sick about me and my sister. There must be a way back."

"Just as you can get here, you can most certainly leave."

"You mean I can go back home?" Webb asked hopefully.

"If that is the way of things, yes. There are four paths out of the Dark Lands and two of them will get you *home*, as you so put it."

"And the other two?"

"The other two will not," Mathias responded curtly. "Reincarnation is perhaps the easiest of the four paths to understand."

"Whoa," Webb interrupted, "reincarnation is for real!?" Then, reconsidering what was going on around him already, he felt a little silly about his outburst.

"Oh, it is very real. Reincarnation is the melding of one's soul, one's essence, to a new body, a new vessel, to accomplish what the old vessel could not."

"You mean people can come back as somebody else to finish what they started?"

"A very simple summary, but an accurate enough one at that," smiled Mathias.

"So all of those people claiming they were Amelia Earhart in their past life were telling the truth?" asked Webb, half-jokingly.

"I am afraid Ms. Earhart was never here in the Dark Lands to begin with, so those people you speak of were either lying or misguided," quipped Mathias. "Nevertheless, we have had many souls leave here to be reincarnated into the living world."

"So, I can just choose to be reborn?"

"In due time, you will have all of your answers. For now, however, it is best that we follow the current flow of our discussion."

Webb didn't appreciate the evasiveness, but he nodded patiently just the same.

"The second path from the Dark Lands—resurrection—is a little more mystifying. This is where the concept of time in the Dark Lands begins to apply."

"You said the Dark Lands is outside of time or something like that," replied Webb.

"But do you understand what being outside of time really means?" Mathias asked with a wry grin.

Webb shrugged. "I don't know."

"What day is it?"

"Uh, I don't remember exactly, but I think it's around February 20th."

"To you, yes. But your uncle doesn't recall the weeks, months, or years you experienced after he died at all. We have others here whose final days were spent in various times in the past—a bitter cold December in 1941, a blistering summer in 1864, autumn harvest season in 1760, and so on. But regardless of the times from their respective lives in the other world, these souls each have the potential to be resurrected back into the living world and resume their lives *exactly* where they left off."

"That's... that's impossible," retorted Webb.

"Is it really? How many near death experiences do you recall reading about or hearing about during your lifetime? How many people resuscitated after being dead for several minutes? Weren't they revived? Weren't they resurrected?" challenged Mathias.

"That's different. Those people were resuscitated. They weren't *dead*. Even if you wanted to put it that way, they were dead for only a few minutes and then came back. They weren't even dead for several hours, much less several years or centuries!" Webb stammered out.

"Are you so certain?" asked Mathias.

Webb looked around the table, seeing his uncle and Iggy watching him intently, before meekly replying. "...No."

"And that is the definition of a timeless realm. You could very well go back and resume your life right where you left it, just as someone who died in 1864 could go back and resume theirs. Here, time is nothing more than a seamless book of infinite pages which can be flipped to and fro. Every second of every lifetime is accessible from the Dark Lands."

"So, I could go back home and it would be as if I never left?"

"Yes," Mathias smiled, "And no one would be the wiser. That is the way of resurrection."

Webb glanced briefly over at his uncle and then back to Mathias. "Why is there both reincarnation and resurrection then? Resurrection seems better."

"'Why' is a word that you need to learn to use a lot less in this realm, Webb, but it's more a practical matter of *how* one died. If the physical death was so violent or terrible that the body was literally rendered uninhabitable, then there is nothing for the essence, or soul, to return to. You cannot resurrect at that point."

"I guess that makes sense," Webb said uneasily, feeling a little sick at the thought and wondering what his own body looked like right now. "...Does anyone ever recall being here? I mean, those who go back?"

"Usually, no. If anything, it's the same tired tale of bright lights and shadowy visages beckoning them onward. Nothing definitive. In that rare event when someone crosses into the Dark Lands more than once..."

"More than once?"

"It happens," Mathias said and nodded. "Sometimes, the soul loses its way when it's returned to the living world and must return to the Dark Lands to be put back on course. Sometimes, the Dark Lands calls them back again. Either way, these few souls do occasionally have more of a recollection than others. They might have a vague remembrance from a past life or some memory burned into them from the Dark

Lands. But again, these instances are few and far between. Besides, not everyone travels the path of resurrection or reincarnation. In fact, a fair majority do not."

"Why?"

"For most, there is no pressing reason for them to return to the living world. It is time for them to move along to the next level."

"What is the next level?" asked Webb.

"The third of the four paths. There are various names that you could call it, if you wanted to get the general idea of it: Heaven is a popular one, but there are many others."

"And the fourth path, does it also take you to the next level?" pressed Webb, intrigued.

It was as if a candle had been snuffed out in an otherwise lightless room. Mathias' demeanor turned very grave, his dear voice heavy and sad. "No, Webb. The fourth path out of the Dark Lands is the most absolute. It is called *the true death*."

"But we just discussed about already being dead. How can we die again?" asked Webb, the words *die* and *dead* stinging a little as he said them.

"I said you suffered a physical death, Webb, nothing more. What is here, now, in the Dark Lands, is what some call the *soul*. I like to think of it as a memory, or echo, of your physical self. But when you experience the true death, even your soul dies. There is nothing left. Complete eradication."

"Nothing is left?" Webb asked.

"Nothing more than a *memory cube* in Remembrance Hall, if you're lucky," Michael whispered solemnly from the background.

Mathias shot him a reproachful look, but quickly hid his displeasure when he saw that Webb hadn't registered the comment.

"I don't *feel* like an echo," Webb said, almost defensively.

"Nor do you look like an echo," Mathias smiled. "If you were to catch your reflection in a mirror, you would see yourself as you last remembered, right down to your favorite clothes."

Webb briefly looked himself over. He hadn't noticed it before, but he was wearing his favorite pair of Levis, a white t-shirt that had always felt "just right" on him, a pair of white Reebok cross-trainers, and, most peculiarly, his blue letter jacket. The jacket had his varsity football letter proudly displayed on the left side and had been his favorite jacket to date—at least until Mary Ellen Moffat, a spiteful ex-girlfriend, had taken and burned it in effigy. But here it was, resting comfortably on his person without a single singe in sight.

Webb looked back up at Mathias. "And my room, here, is it a memory?"

Mathias nodded. "Everyone in Glorian-"

"Glorian?" interrupted Webb.

"*Glorian* is the name of this castle, our fortress within which we safely dwell. Everyone here has their own room and each room is a reflection of where they often felt most comfortable in the living world."

Webb accepted the answer and then looked at his empty plate and glass. "…If we're all just echoes, then why do we need to sleep or eat?"

"The soul needs to be fed and nurtured, just as the body does. Food and sleep are basic representations of these necessities. In reality, what your soul is actually partaking in is much more profound a thing than your conscious mind could easily understand. Therefore, these illusions are used in proxy to facilitate it."

"And the food," responded Webb with a smirk, "I'm guessing it's not always cheeseburgers and french fries then?"

"It is whatever you want, from wherever you want," Mathias answered while eyeing the big cat lying beside the table, licking its lips. "I believe you noticed that the cheeseburger and fries you just devoured… with Gustafson's aid, tasted very much like the fare you once relished at *Lou's* back in your hometown. Michael has often told me about the times that you all shared there previously."

Webb's thoughts drifted slightly at the mentioning of the beloved diner, but he was quickly brought back to reality by the smell of hot fudge. There, miraculously before him now, was the grandest of hot fudge sundaes, overpowered with whip cream, studded with chocolate chips and chocolate shavings. He inhaled the sweet smell again before taking a heaping spoonful of the extraordinary dessert.

"It never ceases to amaze me how the love for ice cream always finds its way here, even in the oldest of souls," said Mathias warmly.

Gustafson, evidently not satisfied with the earlier snack, slowly walked over and began to lick at the whip cream. Webb made a show of trying to shoo the cat away. "Would someone tell me what this giant scavenger is?"

"Gustafson is one of many Felidaes—also called Felixes by some. These creatures reside in the Dark Lands. And they are pretty much the best friends can you have here," replied Mathias, scratching the Felix's ear.

Webb began to ask another question, but was cut off before he could do so.

"It is almost six o'clock, Michael," stated Mathias, suddenly rising from his chair. "Please make sure that Glorian is locked down." He then turned back to Webb. "There will be plenty of time for more questions tomorrow. For now, get a good night's rest." He then silently disappeared into the back of the room with Iggy following close behind him.

Uncle Mike stood. "Let's go, Webb."

Webb stuffed one more serving of the sundae in his mouth before following his uncle out of the room, Gustafson once again at their heels.

After walking silently together for a while, turning down various nondescript hallways, Webb cleared his throat.

"Hey, um... Uncle Mike?" Webb hesitated.

"Hard to say my name isn't it?" the older man laughed. "Hard to believe you're conversing with your dead uncle? You'll become accustomed to it. After a short time, none of this will faze you."

Webb nodded, not knowing if he really believed that or not. "Tell me," he asked looking down at his uncle's walking cane. "You didn't walk with a limp or use a cane, you know... back home. So, why now?"

"Some of us reflect more of the inner self than the outer self, revealing the emotional scars you couldn't see."

"Aunt Cathy?" Webb whispered.

"Yes," he answered with a sad little smile.

"So, there are days and nights here?" asked Webb, rapidly changing the subject. He rubbed his neck, feeling guilty about bringing up his aunt.

"Yes, it helps keep the order of things. Gives people a schedule to work by."

"And what's so special about six o'clock?"

Uncle Mike looked over at his nephew gravely and then continued his staggered gait. "Not everything here is benevolent."

They rounded another indistinguishable stone corner and came upon a giant keyhole. Webb gauged that it had to be at least one foot wide and twice as long. Stranger still was that the keyhole was not part of any doorway he could see; instead, it appeared set into the wall itself.

"Excuse me for a moment, Webb," pardoned his uncle.

Webb watched curiously as he produced a giant burnished black key from a shallow recess within the wall and then inserted it into the keyhole. His uncle turned the enormous key sharply and it stopped with an audible click. Immediately, a low rumble began to fill the castle, sounding and feeling to Webb as if a freight train were passing through the walls around them. After a minute, the noise and vibration stopped and the halls resumed their stoic silence. Uncle Mike pulled the key out of the strange lock and placed it back into the recess in the wall where it rested once more.

"And that's that," declared Uncle Mike.

"What's what?"

"Glorian is locked down."

"From what?" Webb asked. "What's out there?"

Uncle Mike began walking and didn't stop until he reached the door that led to Webb's room. He opened the door for Webb and gestured for him to go inside. "You're inquisitive, Webb. You always have been and that is a good thing. Sometimes, though, you need to be a little more patient. Too much, too soon, can scar you, son. Just go to bed like Mathias told you."

Webb sighed at the reproach.

"I'll tell you this much," his uncle said. "There is a balance here of good and evil. You got a taste of the evil when you and Sundown first arrived and I'm sorry that I wasn't able to spare you from that. As bad as it was though, you've only experienced the tip of the iceberg. There is much more here—on both sides. So much more. You'll find out soon enough.

"Just remember that not everything that happens has an immediate reason behind it. And sometimes even the reasons you do get are not immediately satisfying. Over time though, it all makes sense. Now, get some rest. There's a lot to get accustomed to tomorrow. ...And don't mind the noise."

"What noise?"

After receiving nothing but a silent cursory pat on the back, Webb reluctantly turned around and went into his room, shutting the door securely behind him. He took his jacket off and threw it over the chair at his desk, then sat down sulkily to look around the room, his mind still buzzing with questions. He glanced at the clock ticking away on his book shelf. *What was so big about six o'clock?*

His eyes then fell to his old desk. He could see the various markings and doodles that he'd carved into the plywood with his pencil when he was a kid. He traced the marks with his fingertip—evidence of a time which he was no longer a part of, a life scarcely lived and already lost. The repetitive ticking of the clock only served to emphasize the time gone by. Webb turned to look at it just as the hour struck six o'clock.

Immediately, a violent roar engulfed the castle. Webb watched in horror as the books on his shelf begin to vibrate, and the clock jittered and fell from its place. Muffled screams and low animal moans filled his ears. It was as if thousands of grisly beasts were outside of Glorian, simultaneously shaking and clawing and screeching at the walls. He hurried to his bed to duck under the sheets and tried to cover his ears with his hands, but the sounds would not be abated.

The assault continued for a full hour before the assailants suddenly seemed to evaporate into nothingness, and the quaking and noises ceased as if nothing had happened at all. It took two more hours of stone cold silence and nervous pacing before Webb finally had the courage to turn out his bedroom light and go to sleep.

── CHAPTER FOUR ──

BREAKFAST FOR ONE

Webb awoke early and refreshed. The lethargy that normally dogged him in the mornings was conspicuously absent. He stretched customarily before leaping spryly from his bed and landing in front of his closet door.

Opening it, he was greeted by the cedar-like smell of his mom's laundry detergent. It gave him a moment's pause as the fresh smell washed over him, carrying with it over seventeen years of fond memories. He remembered his dad hunting around for the ever-missing sock, his mom putting the freshly folded linens away in the closet, Sundown rubbing her face into the dryer warm clothes and towels…

He quickly shook off the wave of nostalgia and put on the same clothes he'd worn yesterday and slammed the closet door shut, once again trapping the smell and memories inside. His mom and dad weren't here. But Sundown was; he had to find her. He then left his room to move out into the mammoth stone hallway.

The first thing he noticed was the effusive rich scent of buttermilk pancakes—a welcome contrast to the dank smell of dusty stone and rusty iron that had been so strong the night before. He looked both ways, wondering where the delicious aroma was coming from.

"Webb!" a girl's voice erupted behind him. He turned to see Sundown running towards him, arms wide. Webb met her in mid-stride and heaved her into a bear hug.

"Are you okay?" he asked, setting her down.

"I'm fine," she beamed.

Webb looked up to find a man and a woman approaching behind Sundown, both offering Webb a small, almost apologetic smile. The woman was perhaps the most stunningly beautiful girl he had ever seen. He involuntarily flushed. Her hair resembled spun onyx, shining and sharp, and her ebony eyes glimmered with an unrivaled lustrous chatoyance. She wasn't excessively curvy, but she was nonetheless captivating. He wanted to say "hello" to her, but found his voice lacking. Thankfully, Sundown intervened before the moment became too awkward.

"Webb, this is Raven," she introduced cheerfully. "She was the one who counseled me last night," she introduced cheerfully.

Hoping that he wasn't blushing, Webb took his eyes off of the beautiful woman and managed to refocus on his sister. He was slightly taken aback at Sundown's peppy demeanor, figuring she would be a little more distressed about their present situation. Then again, maybe she didn't really understand their situation. He wasn't even sure if he did.

"And this is Badego," Sundown nodded towards the other adult. Webb's first impression of the man was one of aversion. Badego was a middle-aged mustachioed man. His slacks and collared shirt did no good to hide his lanky limbs and he radiated an insufferable personality through his brushy mustache and wide toothy smile. He reminded Webb of the type who was always overly-cologned who would speak with the self-assured thrust of a door-to-door salesman.

"Hello," Badego said, offering his hand to Webb.

Webb was amazed that the man's voice sounded normal, unlike what he'd been expecting. Putting his initial prejudices aside, Webb shook his hand and smiled. He then immediately turned back to Raven and put on an even larger grin for her. She gave a small nod back, but Webb discerned it to be more of a courtesy than anything else. He flushed red at the realization.

"So, uh, are you hungry, Sundown?" Webb asked, clumsily trying to divert everyone's attentions.

"Are you kidding?" she cried. "That bacon smell is driving me crazy!"

"You mean pancakes," Webb corrected.

"Uh, are you insane?" Sundown argued. "That is *obviously* the smell of *meat*. Bacon."

"We all smell what we want to smell," interceded Raven.

"Should have known," mumbled Webb as they all moved off in the direction of the personalized aromas. "So, where are the smells coming from anyway?"

"The cafeteria," replied Badego.

"There's a cafeteria in the spirit world?" Webb replied absently. He was excited to see the place, hoping it was a little higher class than the cafeteria in his high school.

He didn't have to wait long to find out. The cafeteria defied Webb's expectations. Gone were the folding metal tables, uneven plastic chairs and sticky concrete floors that he'd come to equate with the word "cafeteria." What he saw before him now, he could only describe as a medieval banquet hall crowned with an enormous entryway of sculpted marble.

There were seven long polished wooden tables that stretched the length of the room. Aligned on either side of the dining tables were parallel benches upon which sat men and women of different ages and nationalities. Their visual ages seemed to range from around Webb's age to the very elderly, and Webb imagined that the residents' senses in fashion indicated the decades, or even centuries during which they had lived. Whether dressed in petticoats or bellbottoms, all of the residents were enjoying a very hearty and generous banquet of foods, ranging from the mundane, to the exotic, or bizarre. Despite this sudden confluence of strangers, Webb didn't feel any apprehension and could tell from his sister's countenance that she didn't either.

"Come on, Webb. Let's eat," Sundown grinned. Webb was amazed at her initiative as she led their troupe between two rows of tables to a place right in the middle of the room where four spots awaited, each laid out with silverware and a steaming plate of food.

Sundown instantly took the seat behind a plate heaped with mounds of bacon and eggs. Sunny side up. Webb quickly claimed the plate next to hers that was stacked with butter and syrup-enriched pancakes, the sticky amber rivulets threatening to overflow onto the table. He braced himself. This would not be easy to eat gracefully.

Once settled, he glanced around and saw Raven and Badego taking seats behind plates that had rather meager portions of sausage, eggs and toast.

"After a time, you will become more accustomed to this realm and you will lose your voracious appetite," stated Raven, settling onto the bench beside Webb.

Webb smiled slightly, not sure if the comment was a rebuke or just a simple explanation. He looked over at Sundown. "How'd you know to sit here?"

"Just… mm… seemed… right," she replied mid-chew.

"In the Dark Lands, there is almost an inherent guidance about the place, leading you to where you belong. The longer you are here, the greater your awareness of it will be. Right now, it's probably more hit or miss for you two," offered Badego who was sitting next to Sundown.

Webb gave him a curt nod. Badego seemed nice enough, but there was something just under the surface that made Webb feel uneasy, something that apparently Sundown and Raven didn't notice.

When breakfast was over, they stood to leave the cafeteria. Webb instinctively reached for his plate to clear it away only to find that it had disappeared, as had all the rest of their plates. He jerked his hand back in surprise. Webb caught Raven watching him with a bemused smile and once again felt embarrassed. He looked away and his attention was immediately drawn to the other Glorians that were filing out of the cafeteria.

"Where are they going?"

"Soon, Webb, soon," responded Raven. "Now, however, you should go and meet with your counselor, Mathias." She then turned to Sundown, "If you could meet me in my room in a few minutes, we'll resume our counseling." Raven and Badego then silently headed out with the others.

"Are you *sure* you're okay?" Webb awkwardly interjected as he and Sundown strolled out of the cafeteria.

"Yes, Webb. I'm fine. Everything's good. Don't worry about me."

She smiled at him, but there was a defensive undertone in her response that bothered him. His sister was prone to internalizing her emotions until they became so compounded that she broke down. That would always be the end result eventually and had caused a lot of problems between them in the past.

"This is a lot to take in, that's all I'm saying."

"Webb, I understand. But what you might not understand is that this isn't the end. There are four ways out of here and two of them can take us home. I'm sure Mathias told you the same."

"This is bigger than just going home, Sundown."

"Maybe it's *you* who isn't okay?" Sundown shot back in accusation.

Webb was taken aback at the sudden outburst, but stayed his response. He loved his sister dearly, but she could be as stubborn as they came. "...All right. I just want to make sure you're okay," he finally said.

Sundown's narrowed eyes suddenly darted from her brother's. "Unky!" she screamed, brushing past Webb. Her face shone with sheer joy.

Webb spun around in time to see Sundown leap into Uncle Mike's open arms. *Unky.* He'd stopped calling him that by the time he was ten, but Sundown was still so young when he'd passed; she never grew out of the nickname. The two embraced warmly, reunited after all these years.

"I've been chomping at the bit to give you a big hug!" Michael bellowed out. "Sorry I couldn't do it earlier, but I was engaged with your over-inquisitive brother last night."

"Raven told me you were busy, but I knew you'd come when you had time," Sundown replied excitedly.

"Well, I think you've got an appointment with Raven, so how 'bout I escort you to her room and we can talk on the way to catch up?" Uncle Mike suggested.

"Sounds good!" she beamed. The two began to hurry towards the entry of another hallway, chattering excitedly.

Webb rolled his eyes and sighed. Forgotten before he'd even gotten the chance to open his mouth. "Well, I'll just go to Mathias' alone then. Don't mind me," Webb called after them sarcastically.

"You do that," his uncle shouted back.

"Hope I don't get lost!"

"Just trust your instincts," came his reply from around the corner.

Webb watched them walk off, his uncle's cane still echoing in his ears long after they were out of sight. He then moved off, feeling suddenly very alone.

CHAPTER FIVE

THE WILLKEEPER

Had the walls of Glorian at least a smattering of décor to orient himself by, Webb might have been able to find Mathias' study—but there was nothing except vacant brick and stone and indistinguishable doorways everywhere he turned. There were no numbers, no nameplates, nothing. How could he tell which door would lead to Mathias when they all looked the same?

Frustrated, Webb found himself crossing by the cafeteria for the third time. He looked left, then right, and then left again. Resigned to another fruitless pursuit, he flipped a mental coin and went to the right and wandered down another intersecting corridor. A few steps in, he came across a door that had slowly listed open.

Well, this at least appeared new. He hesitantly approached and peered inside. The room was moody, its only source of light being a small green kerosene lamp resting on the edge of a very busy desk strewn with books and papers. There was also the rich smell of fresh coffee grounds in the air.

"Hello...? Mathias, are you in there?" he called tentatively before immediately regretting the stupid simplicity of the question. When there was no reply, he brazenly stepped inside the large chamber.

It took a moment for Webb's eyes to adjust to the sparse lighting, but then everything came into focus. On either side of the room, extending indefinitely, were shelves packed with books, all bound in dark cherry leather, their spines emblazoned with tiny gold stamp letters. Each book was the size of an encyclopedia, differing only in their respective widths. Some appeared to hold just a few pages while others were hundreds, maybe even thousands of pages thick. He looked around the room for a candle, a flashlight, something that would allow him to examine the books closer, but to no avail. Instead he nosed up to one of the books that fell within the room's limited illumination.

The gold letters were names—one name per book, from what he could see. They were not alphabetized, nor were the books in any other type of discernible order. His curiosity getting the better of him, Webb pulled one off the shelf. The book was heavy, much heavier than its girth betrayed, and its cover very rough, etched with deep lines and creases. The worn leather cover suggested that the book had seen some use. He was just beginning to wonder whose room this could be when suddenly he sensed someone standing behind him.

"Hello," a wavering old Gaelic voice rung out from the far side of the room.

Startled, Webb spun around, accidentally dropping the thick tome on the floor with a resounding thud. His face blanched in mortification. He didn't need to add destruction of property on top of trespassing into the man's chambers. "I'm so sorry," he said, reaching to pick it back up.

Out of the darkness stepped a disheveled figure enveloped in a modest friar's robe; his long-flowing gray hair and beard were unkempt and in desperate need of a comb. "No harm done, boy. That one's been with me hundreds of years. If it isn't broken already, it's not going to be now," the man replied, his robe swishing, the sheen of the fabric alternating between jet black and metallic silver depending on where the light fell upon it.

Webb sheepishly handed the book over to the man. "I'm..."

"You're Webb Thompson," interrupted the man. "Got quite a book on you so far."

"Quite a book?" asked Webb.

"I am the Willkeeper and that is what I do."

"The Willkeeper?"

"Yes," he replied affably.

"Your name is really the Willkeeper?" Webb repeated.

"Yes, just like your name is really Webb." he answered with a chuckle.

"Why not?" Webb said resignedly. "And you have a book on me?"

"But of course I do," guffawed the man, patting the other book and putting it away. He then stretched his hand out towards one of the shelves on the far side of the room. Webb heard something whistle by his ear, followed by the thud of a soft impact. Suddenly, the Willkeeper was holding one of the cherry leather-bound books. He turned its spine towards Webb and handed it to him. It appeared no different from the other tomes, save for the gold foil name running along its spine: *Webb Owen Thompson.*

"Around a good five-hundred pages worth," the Willkeeper grinned before he added, "...so far."

Webb softly rubbed his thumb over his name, feeling the impression of each of the individual letters, in wonderment of what might be written inside. "May I read it?"

"Not now, boyo," the Willkeeper replied, gently pulling the book from Webb's grasp. "Not good to be too engrossed in reminiscing. Poisonous to the soul, if you ask me. Maybe when you've spent more time here, I'll let you have a little peek at its pages."

Webb watched as the book shot from the Willkeeper's hand back into the darkness. "And what do you do again, Willkeeper?"

"I record each and every event that transpires in each and every life. There's a book on everyone who has ever lived, or currently lives, here on these bookshelves."

"And you record all of this by yourself?" Webb asked disbelievingly as he again eyed the scope of the room. "That sounds like an incredible responsibility."

"I sit right there," answered the Willkeeper as he nodded towards the cluttered desk overflowing with sheets and notebooks. "And I write it all down."

"Everything?"

"Everything."

"For dogs too?"

The Willkeeper again extended his arm and another book flew out of the shadows to him. He handed it to Webb.

Webb looked at the spine. "Daisy." He swallowed hard, scarcely believing what he was seeing.

"Yes, she was a good one, lad."

Webb opened the book to reveal pages meticulously inscribed in graceful handwritten script. Skimming through various paragraphs, he found that the words in the records flowed with such introspection and feeling that they became strangely tangible, reeling in his emotions. Somehow, it was as if the words were more than just words, able to transport his mind directly into the depicted scenes. He could see Daisy's dark coat shining under the summer sun as she darted about excitedly in the grass during a romp in the park with him and Sundown. They were all so happy then. Then the book was abruptly shut and Webb felt for a moment as if he'd been kicked in the stomach.

"Too much reminiscing," reminded the Willkeeper as he carefully pulled the book away.

Webb smiled in embarrassment and winced. "Yeah, I think I understand."

"Hello there, Webb," came a voice from behind. Webb looked over to find Mathias standing casually in the doorway.

"Hello there, Mathias," the Willkeeper answered jovially.

"I see you've met our new charge."

"Yes, I was just giving him a small taste of what I do."

"Can't hurt," responded Mathias as he entered the room. "There will be plenty of time later to converse with your new friend, Webb. Now, however, we've questions and answers to attend to."

"Feel free to come back whenever you like," the Willkeeper said, returning to his desk.

"I will." Webb said, waving goodbye as he followed Mathias out of the room. He looked back in time to see the Willkeeper sink back down and begin to write in another one of his countless volumes. Webb couldn't help but feel a little pang of sorrow for him being charged with such a burden.

"I think you brought a little happiness to his day," said Mathias as the two walked away from the Willkeeper's room.

"Doesn't seem like he has much time for conversation, given the nature of his job," replied Webb.

"His task is indeed immense, but I think it is more that others don't have time to see him than the other way around. He gets very few visitors."

Webb felt another twinge of sadness at the implication and made a mental note to make sure to visit the Willkeeper as often as possible. The old man deserved to take a break once in a while even if just to visit with a friend.

As they talked, Mathias walked before Webb, leading him very deliberately down numerous hallways. Webb tried to memorize the twists and turns they took. Left, right, right, left, until he couldn't keep it all straight in his head anymore. He had no idea how he would ever navigate the place.

"Webb. How about we explore around the grounds?" asked Mathias. "You've unfortunately not seen Glorian from the outside, being as you and Sundown were both unconscious when we first brought you here. I assure you, it is quite a sight."

"Sounds like a good idea to me," replied Webb eagerly. The confining stone walls were beginning to wear on him. A stroll outside sounded like a good change of pace.

The pair walked a few minutes longer before encountering a mammoth door, on par with the entry to the cafeteria, except this one evidently led outside.

Mathias turned to Webb and grinned. "Let's take a walk."

CHAPTER SIX

THE VINDICADIVES

"Does the sun ever shine here?" Webb asked as he scanned the horizon. They had only been outside a few minutes, but Webb had yet to see even the slightest hint of sunshine. Only dark clouds, just like when he and Sundown had arrived.

"No," Mathias replied shortly.

"Why?"

Mathias looked at him with a wrinkled smirk. He paused before answering, as if it was the first time anyone had ever asked him the question. "I have always looked upon the dourness of the skies as a warning to us against complacency—a reminder that there is a reason why we are all here."

"And why *are* we here? I mean the Dark Lands isn't exactly something I studied about in Sunday school."

"No, you wouldn't have. As I told you yesterday, the Dark Lands isn't chronicled in your time, or any other time for that matter. To the living world, we do not exist, but without us, the living world would be a smoldering ruin."

"So then," prodded Webb again, "why are we here? Why are we needed?"

"I think you need a little more background here before I come right out and answer that question. But fear not, I shall answer it as much as I am able."

"As much as you're able? What do you mean? And what does any of this have to do with the living world?"

"Come. Let's walk a bit further, to that hillside over there," replied Mathias, brushing off Webb's continuing volley of questions.

Webb looked in the direction where Mathias was pointing, but it all looked the same. Just plain boring grass knolls. He was much more fascinated with Glorian. In his mind's eye, he'd imagined the castle as a leviathan structure with a grid of hallways that stretched for miles north, south, east and west, a perfect stone square amongst a sea of green. From what he could now see, his assessment had been largely correct, save for the sheer magnitude of the structure; its enormity shamed even his imagination.

"Awe-inspiring, is it not?" asked Mathias.

"Yeah."

"Here is a nice spot," Mathias abruptly announced, taking a seat on a hillside. Webb followed his lead and sat down, the grass soft and cushiony like a plush carpet.

They both sat in silence for a moment, gazing upon the fortress Glorian before Webb cleared his throat to remind the old gentleman why they were there.

"Go ahead now," Mathias smiled. "Ask."

"Okay, how did I get here?"

"You mean, *how did you die?*" Mathias clarified.

"Um… yeah," Webb replied uncomfortably. "I can't remember. In fact, the last few days of my life are a blur. I don't have much memory of them. Been that way since I got here."

"No one here knows how they died. When they try and recall it," Mathias made a swooping gesture with his hand, "the memory is unclear."

"Why?"

"It is related to the particular properties of the Dark Lands and its relationship with the time continuum."

"You said this whole place exists outside of time."

Mathias nodded. "Exactly. And because we are outside of time, the lines immediately leading to each of our respective deaths are less than stable. There are just too many vast possibilities, what with resurrection and all."

"But I know how my uncle died. Isn't that a problem then?"

"Do you really know how he died? Think carefully," pressed Mathias.

Webb's face suddenly went blank and he let loose a defeated sigh. "No, it's gone. It's just a blur."

"And that is how it shall remain for now."

"Well, I *do* remember how my Aunt Cathy died," Webb declared defiantly.

"Ah, but she is not in the Dark Lands."

"So, no one here knows how they died?"

"Oh, one person here knows. He knows how everyone died, but he won't tell you either," laughed Mathias.

Webb shook his head. It was pointless. "Who are you, Mathias?"

"I am the oldest person residing in the Dark Lands. Well, the Willkeeper is older, but he is… an anomaly."

"How long has he been here?"

"Since the beginning," responded Mathias.

Realization swept across Webb's face and he let out an involuntary gasp. "What about you? How long?"

Mathias gave Webb a wry grin. That would serve as his answer.

"Fine, I get it," Webb surrendered. He might as well be trying to ask his mother her weight. "What sorts of things can I ask about you, then?"

"I am also a member of the *Glorian Council*," Mathias added. "The ruling body of Glorian. There are seven of us on the Council. We are called *Guides*, and we are responsible for ensuring Glorian's safety and preparedness."

"Preparedness for what?"

Mathias slowly rubbed his bearded chin. "Ah, that is the answer to the question you keep asking—the reason why we are all here."

"Which is…?"

Mathias' demeanor became unexpectedly grave. "You come from a world, Webb, which is rife with those whose souls are filled to the brim, engorged with anger, hate, fear and other such wretched emotions. The living world is plagued by those who would use those emotions to commit atrocities. Those who would do terrible things to other people."

"Yeah, we call them 'insane,'" Webb interjected.

"No, that is not true and you need to appreciate the difference. The truly 'insane,' as you so inelegantly label them, are afflicted with physiological illnesses that preclude rationality."

Webb sighed. "Okay, sorry I called them that. But what kinds of people are you talking about then?"

"The true evil which I am referring to is a genuine affliction of the soul. This decay of the soul is what has long been ravishing the world you know. What is more troubling is that over the centuries, this evil has grown stronger in each successive generation, showing itself at earlier and earlier stages of human development. And the earlier it surfaces in an individual… the more time it has to grow."

"Kind of like lifting weights or something? The more time you have to do it, the stronger you become?" Webb asked, trying to analogize the concept.

Mathias nodded slowly.

"So, what does that have to do with here?" asked Webb.

"These souls I just described don't move on from the living world willingly once their physical shells have died. That world is far too ripe with the rancor and chaos they thrive upon to do that. Instead, these hateful souls, now free of their physical shackles, are able to ravage both the physical *and* spiritual plains. In a word, they are *unleashed*. The Dark Lands exists to remedy that. This place," Mathias swept his arms around grandly, "sequesters those horrid souls. It is like a vacuum—a pull from which they cannot escape."

Webb let his gaze drift slightly over the horizon, watching as the turbulent skies roiled and thundered in the distance. He smelled the metallic tinge of ozone once again, but now it seemed heavier, like a thick coat in his mouth and lungs. *Was that what this place was? One big prison? Was that why he was here? What evil could he have done to deserve being here?* He felt a sickening chill take hold of him.

"Now, the confluence of these souls in the Dark Lands demands a balance. Without that, then even this realm would eventually be overrun and these vile souls would be able to find their way back to the living world. After that, it would just be a matter of time."

"Until what?" asked Webb, fighting through the shock of Mathias' revelation.

"The living world would not last long if the accumulated generations of evil that have collected here throughout all of human history suddenly descended upon it all at once. We are here to prevent that. We, Webb, are the balance—the only thing that stands between *them* and the living world."

Webb felt relieved, knowing he wasn't one of the damned, but it was fleeting and quickly swallowed up by the discomforting knowledge that he was in the proximity of such monsters.

"For every one of the *Vindicadives*," Mathias seemed to spit the word out, "that vomit forth into the Dark Lands, an equally good soul must be sent here to counter it."

"Vindicadives?"

"The evil souls that dwell here," answered Mathias. "That is what they are called. Just as we are called Glorians."

"And so my sister and I are here because there are two more Vindi-whatevers? That's why we're here?" asked Webb.

"There is much more to it than that. Every soul at Glorian has its own unique purpose aside from just providing a universal balance—a purpose that benefits the Dark Lands as a whole. Until that purpose is fulfilled, the soul remains here, in the Dark Lands, unless…" Mathias paused soberly.

"…Unless what?"

"Unless it is cast from this realm by the Vindicadives."

"The fourth way out that you talked about last night," Webb swallowed.

"Yes, the true death," Mathias said darkly. "This is a war, Webb, and the Vindicadives can destroy us just as we can destroy them. Unlike us, however, death is the *only* way the Vindicadives can ever leave the Dark Lands. There are no other paths for them, except if our presence was ever completely removed. Then-"

"They are free to return to the living world to continue their evil," interrupted Webb hastily. "I got that part. But you still haven't really answered my question. Why am *I* here? Why is my *sister* here?"

"I told you that I could answer that question to a point. You are here for a unique purpose and until you accomplish that purpose, here you shall remain. As to the specificity of that purpose, I wish I could tell you, but it is not for me to know. It is just something that plays itself out for each individual Glorian during their time in the Dark Lands. With some, it takes a few years to occur; with others it can take hundreds of years. The key is not to go looking for it. Let *it* find *you*."

"And does everyone eventually end up here? I mean, everyone from my world, err—the living world?" asked Webb, motioning around them.

"No. Most do not. Only certain souls end up here, each with their own proclivity or uniqueness. Most of the others move on to the next level. Theirs is a rather simple transition."

"And in the meanwhile here, each side, the Glorians and Vindicadives, just continues to get bigger?" asked Webb, slightly dejected.

Mathias looked away. "Until recently, yes. However, that has begun to change, all starting with the emergence of the Dark Man."

The words felt to Webb like a drop of ice water had just trickled down his spine. Even the breeze seemed to turn colder. He didn't like the sound of this *Dark Man*.

Mathias noticed Webb's disquiet and put a hand on the boy's shoulder. "His arrival here was heralded like none before him and none since. That was the first omen the Council had that something was different about this soul. You see, normally, when a soul is assimilated into the Dark Lands, the sky momentarily illumes—red if the soul is a Vindicadive, blue if a Glorian. For the Dark Man, there was no such modest warning. He crossed through with an explosion of evil, alerting the entire realm to his presence, daring intercession. It was a frightening display, even to the Council, I might add."

"Do you know who he is, or was?" Webb asked.

"The Willkeeper is the only one who initially knows who crosses through, Glorian and Vindicadive alike, and he always informs us so that we can go and whisk the Glorians to the safety of the castle. But the Dark Man's extreme malevolence completely shadows his identity and actions. His aura cannot be penetrated, not even by the most gifted of Glorians, including the Willkeeper and those of us in the Council."

"What?" Webb blurted. "You have to know *something* about him. What about all those books in the Willkeeper's library? Someone in the living world must have known him; someone's book must have something on him."

"Aside from the fact that he arrived about seventy years ago, we know nearly nothing about him," Mathias stated sadly. "I will tell you though, that whatever his place was in the living world, it must have been terrible. The aura of wickedness that surrounds him is unlike any I have ever seen."

"So where is this Dark Man?" Webb asked anxiously. "He lives here? With us in the Dark Lands?"

"Thankfully, he resides far from Glorian, in the most corrosive corner of the Dark Lands with all of the other Vindicadives. It is a hateful place known as the *Dead Forest of Kenan*."

Webb shook his head. "Sounds terrible. I'd never want to be close to that place."

Mathias paused and then looked ominously towards Webb. "You and your sister were at its very edge."

Webb's stomach tightened. "What are you talking about?"

Mathias wove his fingers together and heaved a low sigh. Clearly, the Dark Man and Vindicadives weren't topics he enjoyed discussing, not matter how many times he had to do it.

"There is an area in the very center of the Dark Lands, a neutral zone where all are birthed into our world, regardless of their allegiance. You and your sister, however, didn't arrive there. You both arrived within close proximity of the Dead Forest, right within the Dark Man's grasp."

Webb's jaw went slack, his mind once again envisioning the wave of slimy monsters coming upon them, the acrid ammonia scent, and how it had burned so badly at the touch. Was that what a Vindicadive was? What they looked like? Sounded like? *Smelled* like? "So, what happened to Sundown and me yesterday, that's *not* the normal welcoming committee?"

"No, Webb. That is why it took your uncle and the other reinforcements so long to get to you. Unfortunately, I fear that such abnormalities will soon become the norm."

"Why?" Webb asked, concerned. "No one should have to go through that."

"I'm afraid it cannot be helped. The Dark Man gained control of all the Vindicadives immediately upon his arrival," Mathias continued.

"Control? He *controls* those things?" Webb asked in horror.

Mathias' face was a rigid mask, teeth clenched in disgust. "Yes. Though the Vindicadives were bad enough back when they were just disorganized packs of mindless animals, they became something far worse under his leadership. And that is how the Dark Lands began to lose its balance. Everything now seems to spiral towards the Dark Man's goal."

"Which is what? What does someone like that want?"

"My peers feel that the Dark Man is no different from his minions, save for his immense power. They feel he is trying to find his way back to the living world, through resurrection or reincarnation, to continue to feed upon it. I am the sole dissenter within the Council on that matter. I think his hunger and ambition go much deeper. I believe that he is trying to physically resurrect himself, as he is now, back into the living world and resume whatever madness he had started there."

"As he is now? You mean with all the powers he has here and his monster army?" Webb inquired.

"That is exactly what I believe. The others on the Council don't concur with my hypothesis for several reasons, all justified of course. For one, no one knows how to go about resurrecting oneself in the manner which I mentioned. It hasn't ever been chronicled in the annals of the Dark Lands; the Willkeeper can verify that. And even if the Dark Man were able to somehow force a resurrection, it would be an entirely different ordeal to recall his time here or to be able to utilize anything he might have learned while here. I have nothing to support my beliefs, save for my own intuition. However, the Council deals only in facts. Therefore, I am outvoted, so to speak."

Webb nodded and rolled over all the information that Mathias had just poured into him. It was a lot to remember and think about. He might have to take some notes when he got back to his room, to keep it all organized.

In the distance, the clouds continued their endless storm, twisted and whipped by the unfelt tempest above.

"Hey, I've got to ask the question, Mathias," Webb said after a while. "When the Dark Man got here, who came through as his balance? Who came to Glorian?"

Mathias turned his eyes down slowly and Webb already knew what he was about to say.

"No one."

CHAPTER SEVEN

THE GRAY BOX

Webb stared at Mathias in disbelief, his heart sinking, but before he could utter a word, the older man was up and already heading back towards the castle.

"Come with me, Webb," he called out.

Their walk was brisk and silent, giving Webb another moment to quietly take in his surroundings. He thought he could make out horses, large black horses, in the distance as they both stepped inside the colossal protective walls of Glorian. He wanted to take a better look at the animals, but he was in a hurry to keep up with Mathias as he wove left and right through a maze of repetitive stony corridors illuminated by similarly identical chandeliers.

"How do you know where you're going?" asked Webb with a slight twinge of frustration. "Everything in this place looks the same."

"Not if you are looking."

"Believe me. I've *been* looking," replied Webb wearily.

"You are still thinking in terms of the living world, a three-dimensional physical world. Just because the space within the Dark Lands appears to be similar to the living world, doesn't mean that it is. Remember, everything and everyone here is just an echo of what once was—something that the more basal primitive part of your soul can understand. The reality is that you now reside in a four-dimensional, sometimes even five-dimensional realm. Navigating from one point to the other in Glorian is as simple as staying focused on… where-you-want-to-go."

Mathias stopped in front of a nondescript door and opened it. His room, the comforting room, unfolded before them. "How was I able to find my room amongst this cavalcade of identical doors? How did I know that this was the one?" he quizzed Webb.

Webb gave an irritated shrug. "I don't know. Because you've been here a while?"

"Because I *wanted* to find it," Mathias corrected. "But give it time and you'll understand," he explained as he welcomed Webb into his chamber. They moved slowly through the room and stopped together before the brightly glowing terrarium that held the gray box he'd seen yesterday.

"You asked who was sent here as a counter for the Dark Man and I told you that no one came through," Mathias recounted.

"You did," replied Webb, his voice entreating Mathias to give further explanation.

"Well, no *one* came through, but this gray box did."

Webb's brow scrunched up curiously and he hunched over to examine the little chest. The humble-looking old box exuded an aura of mystique. The wood was decorated with small carved grooves along every surface— evidence of the meticulous care in its creation. The hinges on its backside, as well as the padlock securing its front, were spackled with crumbling red rust that dulled the tarnished silver beneath it. It must have been crafted some time ago. Webb looked back at Mathias, speechless.

"Look closer."

Webb complied, this time paying closer attention to the light surrounding it. His first impression had been that the glass terrarium that housed the little chest was producing the brilliant glow, but he realized now that he had been wrong. The box itself was shining, the wood almost humming with the golden radiance.

"I don't understand?" asked Webb, stepping back from the strange treasure.

"What is there to understand, Webb?"

"I thought only peoples' souls came through? This is just a box," stated Webb. "...Or am I wrong?"

"No, it is a box, just as you see before you."

"Well, it does have this weird glow," added Webb awkwardly.

"Yes, and *that* is an echo for something else."

"For what?"

"We don't yet know."

"Well, what is inside the box?"

"We also do not yet know that."

"Why not?"

"It has not been opened yet."

"What!? After nearly seventy years? Why *not*?" Webb asked disbelievingly.

"Because it is not yet time for it to open," Mathias replied evenly, shaking his head.

"When *will* it be time, then?"

"When it is time."

Webb felt his eyes begin to cross from exasperation and he groaned aloud.

"This is what we were given in reciprocation, Webb, and it surely has its place in the Dark Lands. Time will reveal the end game. For now, it remains in my guardianship."

"But what about this whole shifting balance thing?"

"The Dark Man has been gradually increasing his ranks over ours with his vile incarnations and has organized the Vindicadives into a consolidated force against us. We don't know how he has done this, nor do we have an appropriate counter."

"And the Vindicadives include are those growling creatures that came after Sundown and me?" asked Webb.

"Those are called Whoop-Dingers," Mathias answered.

"Whoop-Dingers?" Webb repeated incredulously. It didn't seem to match the horrid beasts at all. "Couldn't someone have thought of a scarier name than that? I don't think it does them any justice." Webb grinned nervously, hoping for some levity in their rather gloomy conversation.

Mathias was not amused. He shot Webb a cold look that could've melted ice and then freeze it again.

Webb swallowed at the reproach and nodded sheepishly for Mathias to continue.

"Jokes aside, the Whoop-Dingers are indeed part of the Dark Man's arsenal, but they are not Vindicadives. Vindicadives are malignant souls. Whoop-Dingers are…something new. Their task is to seek out Glorians and engulf them, to transform them."

"Transform them?"

"Into more Whoop-Dingers. It is a horrible process—one that I have unfortunately witnessed too many times, and one that would have befallen you and your sister had Gustafson not intervened when he did."

Webb shivered, the weight of Mathias' reprimand now taking on a new meaning. Is that how close it had been?

"The Dark Man has other such vile creatures—Menschenklaus and Whisperers among them, all ruthlessly honed for the depletion of our ranks."

"Well, take out some of those Whoop-Dingers and whatever else then," spoke Webb adamantly.

"It is not that easy. Not only are they dangerous to pursue, they rarely stray from Kenan long enough for us to seek them out to destroy them. And going into the Dead Forest is impossible. That place drives all who enter from Glorian mad with its twisted malevolence."

"Well, they sure seem to be afraid of cats," replied Webb, recalling how Gustafson had so easily chased the entire troupe of Whoop-Dingers away.

"The Felidaes? Yes, they have that effect on all of the Dark Man's manifestations."

"Why? What's so special about Gustafson and the other Felidaes?" Webb asked. "Other than being so huge, that is."

"Felidaes are the one creature that can cross between worlds at will. The same laws that apply to you and me in the Dark Lands do not apply to the Felidaes. They are the closest to divinity that you will ever come across here. And because of that, they are feared by the Dark Man and his followers."

"Then why don't you use them to attack-"

"Because *that* is not their purpose," interrupted Mathias, an edge to his voice.

Webb paused in thought. This was trying. "…Let me get this straight. So, *they* attack and *we* defend," Webb finally said bluntly.

"Mind your tone, Webb. But, to answer you shortly: yes."

"How does that make any sense? Aren't we all just sitting ducks, then?" Webb cried.

"We are not as helpless as your 'sitting ducks,' Webb. We have Glorian to protect us and we wait. There are certain points in which we can counterattack. These turning points are called *thousand-year wars*." Mathias' voice was very low as he peered deeply into the boy's unconvinced eyes.

"What is a thousand-year war?" asked Webb, his indignation retreating at the somberness in Mathias' tone. *This would not be good.*

"About every thousand years—a thousand *living* years, mind you— the Dark Land's tolerance for Vindicadives reaches its peak, the point of spiritual saturation at which a cleansing must take place. A war thus begins to mitigate the overload of souls in the realm.

"You mentioned battles, Webb. The thousand-year wars, a couple of which I have unfortunately participated in, dwarf any battle in the history of the living world. You cannot begin to fathom the carnage that ensues. In their wake, nothing remains but true death for the unlucky and despair for the rest. For if the Vindicadives were ever to prevail, the Dark Lands would be overrun and the living world would soon follow its dismal fate. Conversely, all a Glorian victory has ever secured is a guarantee that there will be another war in another thousand years. Is that the type of battle you seek?" asked Mathias in a haunted tone.

"Seems pointless, all of it," Webb replied under his breath. "That isn't fair."

"The desire for battle no longer as strong, is it? The lust for battle is always strongest in those who have never experienced its bloodshed. It is important that you remember that, Webb. Our place in the Dark Lands is one of extreme importance. Just because we do not attack mindlessly like the Vindicadives does *not* mean that we are weak."

The admonishment stung, more so because Webb knew he deserved it. It made him feel very embarrassed and, suddenly, very tired.

"I think we are finished for now," announced Mathias, sensing his young charge's lethargy.

"Do I have to go to my room again?" he asked, half-serious.

Mathias smiled a little. "Spend the rest of the day familiarizing yourself with Glorian. Take a walk around, inside and out. Talk to people. It'll make you feel better. Just remember to stay well within the walls during the six o'clock hour."

"What happens at six o'clock? I heard screams last night and everything was shaking."

"Six in the evening is the Dark Man's hour. It is when his manifestations lay siege to Glorian. They try and find ways through our walls."

"That's awful!" Webb gasped. "What are we supposed to do?"

"Do not fear; they cannot breach our walls. It is more a show of intimidation than anything else. The attacks are very consistent and we can prepare for them easily. The foreboding and helplessness associated with the assaults can wear on some residents' morale, however. It is a psychological technique that has been used in many wars."

"Um, I'll just stay in then," Webb hurriedly replied.

"No," Mathias countered. "You really should go out in the later hours and look upon the skies of the Dark Lands at night. It's quite spectacular. Just do it after the clock strikes seven and the attacks stop."

"Okay, so what happens tomorrow?" queried Webb.

"Tomorrow is the first day of the rest of your existence here, Webb Thompson. Tomorrow you will discover your *gift*."

CHAPTER EIGHT

IGGY

Webb's head felt congested, the barrage of information Mathias had just pounded into him knocking about in jumbled pieces. He'd had questions he wanted answered, but getting the answers from Mathias was like trying to get a sip of water from a fire hose. And on top of it all, Mathias had thrown in a new wrinkle with his talk of a "gift."

The old man had alluded to the therapeutic qualities of wandering the Glorian grounds. Well, Webb needed some kind of a distraction. Maybe that would help. Sundown might appreciate the excursion as well. He'd have to invite her. But first, he needed to eat; he was starving again already. Webb figured his appetite stemmed from the stress of learning everything. Raven said it would abate with time. Maybe so, but for now he was famished.

He glanced ahead and saw a lone figure standing immobile in the hallway. At first he didn't recognize who it was—no surprise, given that he hadn't met that many people since his arrival. Then, he saw the tatty teddy bear dangling from the figure's right hand.

"Iggy?"

Iggy smiled in acknowledgement.

"What are you doing?"

Iggy just continued beaming while his sandy head lulled from side to side, as if he didn't know what to say, or how to say it.

"Shy, huh? Hey, I'm going to get something to eat," said Webb, taking the initiative. "Do you want to come with me?"

Iggy stopped his nervous head gestures and surprised Webb by stuttering out, "Th-Thank you, Webb."

Webb contained his shock at actually hearing the man's voice; he was beginning to think that he was a mute or something. He nodded to the young man and took the lead around the corner. He was then met with another surprise: the entry to the cafeteria. He'd actually found something this time without stumbling over himself or going around in circles.

It was not as full as it had been at breakfast time, but the aroma of varied foods circulating the enormous chamber was just as enticing. He could smell the meals that the other residents enjoyed as he walked by—burgers, succulent pies, soups, and even a hint of sweet cornbread. Webb instinctively walked through the cafeteria and stopped before an unclaimed plate at one of the center tables where a large pepperoni pizza, New York deli style, had materialized. He sat down and looked over to where Iggy was sitting across from him, a decadent chocolate chip cake in front of the man.

"Quite the nutritional lunch there, Iggy," commented Webb as he watched the man gingerly set his ragged teddy bear beside him and proceed to take huge bites out of the cake. Webb was impressed that despite the man's ravenous appetite, he was very careful and not a single crumb was spilled, and no mess made. In between bites, Iggy managed to give Webb another of his infectious smiles; even his shining blue eyes seemed to smile at him. Webb had never met someone who radiated such sincere joy. It was refreshing just being around him.

"Hey, Iggy. You don't talk much, do you?" asked Webb as he took a bite out of his pizza slice, enjoying the tastes of the melted cheese, pepperoni, and savory tomato sauce blending in his mouth.

"No, he doesn't."

Webb felt a finger slide across his back before Raven sat down beside him and offered a polite smile. A blush of red rushed to Webb's cheeks, making him look away, flustered. *Why couldn't he contain his composure around her?* He was acting like a silly love-struck teenager. Well, he *was* a teenager, but he was far from love-struck. However gorgeous she was, he barely even knew the woman and she was probably thousands of years his elder anyway. *Now that*, he mused, *was pretty funny.*

Webb's then received a sudden kiss to the top of his head. He looked around to find Sundown moving past him and taking a seat next to Iggy, a plate full of peanut butter sandwiches and Cheetos before her. He almost cringed at the abominable combination.

"Hi!" she greeted Webb cheerfully.

"Hi, Sunny," Webb replied, happy to see her as well.

She turned to Iggy. "Hello, my name is Sundown. What's your name?"

The round man stopped eating his cake and looked towards her. He gave her a small perplexed look, as if he was confused by the question. He then wiped his lips, though there was not a trace of cake or icing on it, and attempted to mouth something to Sundown, but nothing audible emerged. Finally, he just smiled at her shyly and stuck his hand out in greeting. Sundown shook it eagerly, showing no disquiet at the man's bizarre behavior.

"His name is Iggy," answered Raven.

Webb didn't know if Iggy really registered that Raven had introduced him, but his face did seem to brighten slightly at the sound of her voice.

"So, Raven," asked Webb, getting the courage to address her, "Why is Iggy-"

Raven quickly slapped her hand on his thigh underneath the table, silencing him. Webb looked into her piercing glare and got the message. *Some questions were best asked in private.*

"Why is Iggy what?" asked Sundown.

Iggy seemed inquisitive as well, wondering where the discussion was heading.

"Eating cake. Why is Iggy eating cake?" Webb recovered lamely. He felt like kicking himself.

Iggy beamed again and resumed his eating. Webb noted that he was almost half way through the dessert with still no sign of slowing down.

"Sundown, perhaps you can answer your brother's question?" replied Raven. There was a slight, almost imperceptible, leer in Webb's direction, a silent rebuff for his earlier breach of etiquette.

"Webb, it doesn't matter what we eat here as long as we eat. The food is just a comfortable recollection, something we can accept. What we're really ingesting is way beyond explanation, or at least that's what Raven told me," Sundown answered smugly, feeling that she'd gotten the better of her older brother.

"Yes, apparently word-for-word," replied Webb in annoyance.

"Your sister is quite the learner, Webb. You should be proud of her," chastised Raven. She gave him another funny look and Sundown giggled.

Webb felt like he was the brunt of another joke. His immediate inclination was to rise from the table and leave everyone to their snickering, but he thought better of it and just smiled sardonically.

"Although, Mathias does speak highly of you as well," Raven added.

Webb gave an unenthused nod in her direction. "So, where is uh, Badego?" he asked, not missing the used-car salesman lookalike, but wanting to get the conversation as far away from his asinine "cake" question as possible.

"He is off doing his own tasks, tasks you will both become familiar with in due time. He joined us this morning just to introduce himself. I am the counselor for Sundown, just as Mathias is yours. It is a one-to-one tutorial, if you will."

"Are you excited about tomorrow, Webb?" asked Sundown as she scarfed down another peanut butter sandwich. It looked to Webb as if she were on her third one.

"What happens tomorrow again that I should be excited about?" replied Webb, drawing a blank.

"Our *gifts*! We get to discover our gifts," Sundown replied spiritedly.

"Oh yeah," he replied casually. He had tried to push that concern aside for a while and hoped his cool response was enough to cover his anxiety. He wasn't sure if these "gifts" were necessarily something to look forward to like Sundown was. Webb had a feeling it wouldn't be anything like a birthday present; he figured it would be more like they'd be given tools to do chores around the castle or get magical soul papers to be officially drafted into the next war.

"It is one of the more important things you'll discover here, Webb—if not the most important," added Raven. She then leveled her gaze at Sundown. "These gifts can save lives. I think you might appreciate that fact, young lady."

Webb noted a transitory exchange between the two, a look that harbored a secret. As much as Webb wanted an explanation, he didn't bother to intrude. *Women.* Instead, he turned his attention quietly back to his pizza.

When everyone had finished with lunch, they departed the cafeteria, Webb in awe that Iggy had eaten his entire cake clean. For some reason, it made Webb feel good. Watching Iggy stride ahead and out into the hallway with his teddy bear in hand, Webb was struck with a sudden fraternal instinct and he began to follow after him.

"He'll be okay, Webb," stated Raven, grasping Webb's arm to stop him.

When she let go, the place where she'd grabbed his wrist tingled slightly and he rubbed the spot.

She then said to Sundown, "The rest of the day is yours, Sunny. Do what you want."

Webb spoke up. "Hey, I'm going to look around Glorian. Maybe take a walk outside. Want to come with me?"

"Sure!" Sundown beamed. "I'll go get ready. Meet you at your room in a few minutes." She then turned and hurried off down the hall.

Webb was about to say his goodbyes to Raven when she put a finger to his lips. "You wanted to know about Iggy? Why he is the way he is?"

He nodded.

"Mathias told you that we are all echoes of our former selves, yes?"

"Something like that."

"Well, the echoes are reflections of our true selves and sometimes our true selves bear scant resemblance to what we were like in the living world."

"Kind of like the old saying, *it's what's on the inside that counts?*"

Raven smiled at the proverb, causing a flutter in his chest. "Yes, there are beautiful people with ugly hearts and malformed people with beautiful hearts. Iggy was one of the latter."

"That's why Iggy is so… distant?" Webb asked, rubbing his head and trying to look away from her lips. *Distant* really wasn't the word Webb was looking for, but it was the best one that came to mind.

"Iggy had a severe condition and was mentally retarded in the living world. It is his heart that you see here now. However, some of the shadows from his worldly affliction followed him through to here."

Webb was speechless from surprise and embarrassment, suddenly feeling insensitive in the way he'd been speaking to him. It all made sense to now: the reluctance to speak, the sweet child-like disposition, the awkwardness.

"His story is one of the saddest ever to broach the Dark Lands. I cannot tell it without my own heart breaking. Maybe one day you'll know his story, but not this day." She offered a sad smile to Webb and then, inexplicably, she softly kissed his cheek.

Webb felt no sensuality in the kiss, only warmth and a sharing of sadness from one soul to another, but the act itself still gave him a moment's pause. "Why is he here then, Raven? Why does he have to go through all this?"

"Everyone has a purpose," she replied before silently walking away.

CHAPTER NINE

THE MURADIANS

Ten minutes later, Sundown was at Webb's door with her bubbly enthusiasm shining in her eyes. She'd gone back to her room to change for their adventure outside and was now in a pink windbreaker and jeans.

"Your room! It's your room!" she squealed as she hurried in and began spinning around and around, taking in everything she could.

"Yes it is," he replied amusedly.

"Isn't it amazing?" she said as she ran her fingers over his desk, bed, dresser, every piece of the room she could touch. "It's just like home!!"

But it isn't home, he thought to himself. Webb said nothing to her; he didn't want to put a damper on the moment. He just watched as she picked up his books, glanced over his football trophies, and even took a deep breath inside his closet. Then she looked back towards the bedroom door and her cheerful expression faded.

"I just want to open that door, Webb. I want to open that door, go down the hall into Mom and Dad's room and hug them, hug them until they *know* I love them."

Webb walked over to her and held his sister tight. "They knew you loved them, Sunny. You don't ever need to worry about that…"

"Let's go outside," she said abruptly, rubbing her eyes.

Webb nodded. *Same ol' Sunny, an island unto herself.* "Very well," he said with a mock bow. "After you, my lady."

A few turns later, they found the door to the outside. Sundown had led the way and had found it effortlessly.

They pushed through the massive wooden entry doors and were soon traipsing across the grounds, Sundown leading the way. Strangely, it appeared to Webb that the grass in his sister's wake was springing back up almost instantly, unscathed. He looked back and saw that it was doing the same with his own footsteps. He knelt down and pushed his hand down firmly against the soft green blades. At first, there was a definable handprint when he raised his hand, like a depressed piece of soft foam, but then the grass quickly sprang back up, erasing the impression—amazingly resilient. He wondered if that was an echo for some quality, like the resilience of nature or something.

Webb moved to call Sundown's attention to this when he noticed that she had stopped, her gaze focused intently on the skies. He slowly walked up beside her and joined her in silence, both pair of eyes looking heavenward.

At points along the horizon, the sky held flat and gray, at others there were thunderheads and swirls of angry weather. On occasion there would be a brief spattering of lightning in the distance, followed by a low rumble of thunder.

"Do you find it peaceful or frightening?" Sundown finally asked.

"A little bit of both, I guess."

"I just find it peaceful. Don't you think it's pretty?"

"It is kind of pretty," Webb offered.

"I've never seen a sky like this before," she commented. "The clouds are amazing."

Webb nudged her. "Hey, speaking of amazing, come with me; I've got something I want to show you."

She turned to him excitedly. "What is it?"

"Just follow me," Webb replied secretively as he turned away and began walking parallel to Glorian.

"Hey, c'mon tell me!" she prodded. "At least give me a hint!"

Webb just laughed and sped up to a jog. Sundown followed, peppering him with questions all the while, but she knew it was pointless to expect a response when he was playing at this game. Webb was good at keeping secrets and often tormented her by withholding them until the last possible moment. Finally, after following the fortress wall for many minutes, Webb found what he was looking for, just beyond a small, gently sloping valley in the distance.

"So, what did you want to show…" Sundown's voice caught in her throat at the sight before their eyes.

Webb turned with a smile. "I saw them earlier, but I wasn't quite sure what they were. Thought I'd hedge my bets."

"They're beautiful," gasped Sundown as she gazed upon the most amazing horses she had ever seen.

Their skin, manes, hooves, every part of them was a pure effusion of crystalline darkness as if they had been born out of resplendent obsidian itself. Some were standing patiently, nipping the grass beneath them, while others jostled around each other in playful jest. A few seemed to be staring at Webb and Sundown, their tails twitching with unease.

"I have never seen anything more beautiful," Sundown declared with tears welling in her eyes.

"I thought you'd appreciate this," replied Webb, breathing a silent sigh of relief that his gamble had paid off. He hadn't gotten a good look before, and he would have been quite embarrassed had the black things he'd seen earlier turned out to be cows or trees. Riding horses had been a passion of Sundown's. For her eighth birthday, their mom and dad had bought her a horse and she'd spent almost all of her free time since riding and taking care of him. Until now that was.

"Thank you, Webb," Sundown replied, the tears now spilling from her eyes.

Webb was feeling so good about the moment, taking in the sight, that he didn't notice his sister advancing on the horses until she was far ahead of him.

"Sundown, what are you doing?" he called after her. He spoke softly so as to not spook the animals. Before he could do anything more, she was already standing just a few feet from one of them.

Several of the more skittish horses had moved clear of Sundown, but the one she had directly approached held its ground. With Sundown standing there amongst them, she could now fully appreciate the creatures' enormity as the animals towered several feet above her head. Their anatomy was fairly consistent with that of a Clydesdale, but their coats were flawlessly smooth as glass, with an unadulterated black sheen. Their eyes too were pitch black, with no distinction between the sclera, iris or pupil. It might have looked more frightening if they weren't so beautiful.

She moved forward slightly and reached her hand out, holding it flat before the horse's nose. The creature snorted and hesitated momentarily before sniffing it. The horse then let out a slight whinny and moved closer to Sundown, lowering its head in apparent submission. Sundown began to caress the animal's face lovingly while gently pressing her cheek against its gleaming skin.

Webb had witnessed the entire exchange on pins and needles, heart in his throat, and now that Sundown was actually touching the behemoth, his apprehension wasn't lessening. Maybe it had been a bad idea to bring her here. They were new to a strange land full of strange beasts; they had no idea if the animals were dangerous or not. Even worse, the rest of the herd was slowly beginning to converge on her. That couldn't be good.

Sundown looked over happily and signaled for Webb to join her. He shook his head adamantly and conversely motioned for her to return to his side.

Frustrated, Sundown yelled out, "Ugh! Webb, come here already!"

The shout startled him and he hoped with bated breath that it didn't intimidate the animals. He glanced nervously at the other horses that were still closing in on her. "Sundown, get away from them and get back over here!" he cried back softly.

Instead of complying with her brother's well-meaning intentions, she did something that gave him further cause for alarm. She whispered something into the horse's ear and in one fluid motion, it bowed forward and Sundown climbed onto its back. The animal then rose and began galloping towards Webb. All Webb could do was stare in amazement, a smile finally breaking through his concern.

"This is PJ," Sundown said casually as they came to a halt before Webb. "He's a *Muradian*."

"Um… Did he tell you this?" Webb asked, nodding in the horse's direction.

"Nooo," replied Sundown, her eyes rolling in mock indignation. "I just *named* him PJ. And these horses are *called* Muradians, silly."

"How could you possibly know that they're called Muradians?" asked Webb. "You didn't even know they existed until just now."

"I knew they existed. Raven told me about them. I told her how much I loved horses."

"Oh," Webb nodded, feeling slightly sour that Raven had spoiled his surprise. *Well*, he thought, *she really didn't. She only told Sundown about the horses; I was still the one who showed them to her.*

"They've lived in the Dark Lands forever—one of the oldest creatures around. Fastest creatures around too! Legend has it, if they go fast enough, they'll leave a trail of fire behind them," she added.

"So, are you the Dark Lands historian now?" asked Webb sarcastically.

"No, I just listen, unlike *some* people," Sundown retorted. "Now, let's go for a ride."

"I don't think so. You're the equestrian in the family. I'll just sit on the grass and wait-" Webb was suddenly nudged forward in mid-sentence. He lurched around to find that another Muradian had wandered up behind him and was presently staring him down with its big dark eyes.

"He wants you to ride him," laughed Sundown.

"And how do you know that?"

As if on cue, the Muradian bowed forward, exposing its long powerful neck for him to climb. Webb looked from the horse to Sundown and then back to the horse. This was his fault. Had he not shown her the horses, she wouldn't be begging him now to go riding with her. As his mom always said: *"You made your bed, now lie in it."*

"Okay, how do I get on this thing?" Webb conceded with a sigh.

"He is not a thing; he is a horse," Sundown corrected. "Just climb over his neck and he'll do the rest."

Webb, feeling uncertain about the whole venture, slowly lifted his left leg over the horse's neck and gently climbed upon it, trying to get comfortable. Swiftly, the horse lifted upright, sliding Webb onto its broad muscular back. Webb quickly wrapped his arms around either side of the horse's neck and readied himself for the disastrous fall he was certain would occur at any moment.

"Great... Now what?" asked Webb.

"Let's ride around," she beamed.

"I don't know if you noticed this, but these horses don't have saddles, much less reins."

"We don't need saddles or reins, big brother." Sundown gently tapped the sides of PJ with her feet. With that, the horse began to trot forward with Sundown perfectly astride, her hands barely grazing the sides of his neck.

Webb, swallowing the knot of trepidation in his throat, lightly tapped the sides of the horse and the Muradian began to move forward. Following his sister's lead, Webb loosened his grip and placed both hands to either side of the animal's neck, albeit with less confidence and poise. For all of the creature's huge size though, Webb was amazed out how smooth the ride was, and how graceful. He thought that the Muradian would surely knock him off once it started trotting around and that the ride would be terribly uncomfortable and bumpy. It was none of this; instead Webb felt very much at peace atop the horse.

"You really ought to give your Muradian a name," Sundown said once Webb had edged up beside her.

Webb glanced over at his sister, so tiny upon the great animal. "Um, he's not *mine*," he said with a hint of annoyance. It was difficult to focus on looking at her and keeping balanced while on the horse's back. Didn't she realize he couldn't talk and ride at the same time?

"Well, I think he likes you."

Webb laughed. "I think he just wanted some exercise."

Sundown smiled and took in a deep breath. "Thank you again, Webb. I needed a moment like this."

Webb just grinned back. There was nothing he needed to say.

For a long while, they rode side-by-side in silence over the rolling hills and flat plains that stretched on forever. For a time it seemed as if they were gently traveling over a vast green ocean. Every once in a while, a show of lightning would play in the distance, adding to the maritime illusion.

A slight brush of moisture across his cheek made Webb look around. A dense wet fog had suddenly come upon them, radically limiting their view to less than a hundred yards. The change, however, didn't unnerve them or the animals and despite Webb's better judgment, they kept their course.

Webb took in a deep breath of the cool vapor and exhaled, watching his breath play upon on the mist before dissipating into the rest of the fog. It felt nice. He slowly crooked his head around, a strange feeling beginning to envelop him.

"Sunny, do you feel…"

"…like I've been here before," she completed.

"Weird," Webb mumbled.

It was as if the perfect mixture of contentment and sleepiness had suddenly been poured over him—the feeling of soaking in a hot bath on after a long day, or laying down to rest after a big Thanksgiving dinner. He heard Sundown say something else, but the words were too droned out to be discernible, as if she were speaking from far away. All he knew was that he hadn't felt this at ease in a long time and he didn't want the moment to end.

Webb had no idea how long they plodded forward, each step feeling like they were moving deeper and deeper into warm molasses. Caught somewhere between lazy wakefulness and early sleep, Webb noticed nothing of his surroundings until, by chance, his head bobbed upward and he caught sight of something breaking through the fog, interrupting the misty serenity.

Several shapes slowly began to materialize in the distance. Webb squinted his eyes to try and focus the image, but either his tired eyes wouldn't work properly, or the shapes refused to be defined. From his limited perspective, they looked like long, floating, hourglass formations.

"Sundown, do you see them?" he asked.

She looked up groggily, Webb's voice bringing her out of her own discombobulated state. "...What are they?"

"I don't know," Webb replied absently. A pink hue was now starting to creep in from behind the forms.

It then dawned on Webb that the shapes were shadows, shadows that were cascading and bouncing around within the wavering pink light. Looking deeper, he could just make out the forms from which the shadows originated. They looked human, but gaunt and dry, as if mummified. Webb started in his seat and began to pull back, but just as quickly, he was again overwhelmed by the feelings of comfort and acceded to moving forward.

Sundown, on the other hand, had never faltered in her course. The peacefulness of that rosy light was where she wanted to be. That was her focus. She hastened PJ forward, but the Muradian would not comply. Slightly aggravated, she urged him forward again, her feet tapping PJ's sides much harder this time, but still the great animal refused. Angrily, Sundown swung her right leg over PJ's back and slid off of him. She began to walk forward when something jerked her back forcefully. She turned her head to find PJ had latched tightly upon her jacket with his teeth.

"Let go, let go!" she implored frustratingly, but PJ would not submit.

The horse glared at her with its big round eyes and snorted in distress.

Grunting, Sundown ripped the coat free from the PJ's mouth, leaving shreds of the pink fabric still caught in his teeth. Hurriedly, she continued towards the pink light, filled with an ache of unbearable longing.

"SUNDOWN! WEBB! BACK AWAY!" a voice cried out.

Sundown shook her head in confusion. She looked back through the fog and saw Uncle Mike sitting on another Muradian, his gaze intently fixed on her.

"Come here, Sundown. *Now*," he said sternly. "Webb, you too."

Webb blinked his eyes rapidly and then took another deep breath. He felt strangely upset, as if he'd been awakened from a pleasant dream prematurely. Blearily, he turned his Muradian around and angled towards his uncle, the sweet sensation of contentment dwindling the further away from the light he moved.

"Get on your Muradian *now*, Sundown," he heard their uncle call out. Webb turned to find Sundown on foot, reluctantly guiding PJ behind her.

"…His name's PJ," Sundown replied sullenly as she mounted the horse.

"Let's get out of here and back to Glorian," Uncle Mike ordered as he circled around the pair, making sure they both were in front of him. He then hurried them along, creating distance between themselves and the analgesic light.

It took several minutes before Webb was able to find his voice again and manipulate his lips to ask the question that had been burning inside of his skull. "What was that place, Uncle Mike?"

His voice was solemn as he looked at Webb and said, "The Requiem."

CHAPTER TEN

THE REQUIEM

"What's the Requiem?" Webb asked.

"Just keep moving," Uncle Mike replied gruffly.

Webb wanted to ask the question again, but his uncle's curt demeanor recommended otherwise. Instead, he just kept his attentions alternating between the ground in front of him and Sundown to his side as she slumped feebly against PJ.

"It's a window," Uncle Mike suddenly announced once they were clear of the fog.

Webb and Sundown simultaneously looked over at their uncle, his response pulling them both from their groggy malaise.

"A window?"

"A window to the living world," Michael clarified. Reading the puzzled looks Webb and Sundown were giving him, he continued. "Just a window. Sounds harmless enough, doesn't it?"

The siblings made a half-hearted attempt at a nod..

"Well, it is far from that, and you two would be best advised to stay away from it," he said severely, surprising his niece and nephew with his fierce warning. "I'm sorry," he quickly added, feeling guilty for startling them, "but you have to appreciate the dangers."

In truth, Michael was glad his voice had made them jump, even if he felt a little bad about it. It let him know that they could understand him and that they weren't still under the Requiem's deadly influence.

"But how can looking back home be bad?" asked Sundown.

Uncle Mike nodded sadly. "True, it does give you a view back into the living world. Specifically, back into your own life. Every single moment is there, day by day, like a diary or scrapbook. But that is just a trick to bait you. It turns cruel soon enough, showing you the living world moving along without you. Family, friends, all living their own lives, the void where you once were quickly dissolving. But by then, it is far too late to look away. You are trapped."

"How do you become trapped?" Webb felt a slight chill at the thought of watching his own life pass before his eyes, much less continuing on without him.

"You saw the shadows there, in the light?"

"Yes."

"They are souls just like us—or at least, they used to be," Uncle Mike said darkly. "You see the Requiem survives off the energies contained within the soul. Once you cross into its threshold, it wraps around you, entangles you, sucks the very essence out of you. From that point forward, you're like a fly trapped in a spider's web, hollowed out beyond any chance of recovery. That's what would have befallen you two, had you entered." He paused and looked at Webb and Sundown's unsettled expressions.

"I had no idea, Unky," Sundown murmured.

"If you look into the Requiem long enough, you can see them, you know?"

"See what?" asked Webb.

"Those souls, the ones the Requiem trapped. Their lifeless eyes staring out into nothingness, bodies emaciated and intertwined within the mists of the Requiem as it feeds upon them. But as grisly as that sight is, what the interned soul itself must endure is much worse."

Webb steadied himself on his Muradian. "What could be worse?"

"Living eternally as a ghost."

"What do you mean a ghost?"

"We call them *sulkers* in the Dark Lands, the souls in the Requiem. But in the living world, they are known as ghosts, forever watching sadly as the living world moves along without them, while their soul rots in the Requiem.

"Every once in a while, someone in the living world will catch a glimpse of them, report it as a haunting or some such."

Sundown felt her heart breaking. "So, there's no hope for them?"

"None," their uncle replied.

No one said anything for the next few minutes. The only sound was the whispering of the Muradians' footfalls on the soft grass.

"...Uncle Mike?" asked Webb, finally breaking the silence. "How did you know to find us there?"

"Because everyone eventually finds themselves at the Requiem. It is inevitable. Even when we warn people away from it, their curiosity will always draw them in sooner or later. It is the proverbial *Forbidden Fruit* of the Dark Lands."

"You could always just put a guard there or something," proposed Webb.

"Did you not feel how powerful its pull was? It lured you both in and neither of you were the wiser. Anyone even remotely close to the Requiem is susceptible to its temptations, and it becomes worse the longer you are exposed to it, poisoning your soul more and more. Posting a guard would be impossible," he retorted.

"Why would something like that even *be* here then?" asked Webb disgustedly.

"It's just another reflection, Webb—an echo perhaps of our envy at not being able to live forever, envy at life continuing on without us, envy at a lot of things," Michael shrugged.

"Sounds like an echo of one of the Seven Deadly Sins," Webb added.

"You're learning," the older man replied.

"Any *more* surprises?" asked Sundown as a loud burst of lightning made her flinch.

"Too many too discuss in one setting, Sundown. As time goes on, you will learn more," he replied absently, giving the sky a hard look.

It wasn't the response Sundown wanted, but her experience with the Requiem had drained her to the point where arguing was not a viable option. She was exhausted. The thought of lying down in her bed was what currently engaged her, made more desirable by the fact that the skies were suddenly darkening.

"*Nightfall*," Uncle Mike hissed. "Mother of all that is merciful..."

There was a sudden convergence of darkness over the horizon, like a cloud of ink had been spilled in the sky, surging throughout their entire field of view as if flowing through a liquid medium. Webb looked nervously to his uncle.

"*We're on the cusp of six o'clock*. How could I be so stupid?!" Michael spat out.

"Six o'clock," Sundown gasped.

Their uncle sat erect on the back of his Muradian and tightened his grip on the horse's thick locks. "We have to make a run for Glorian."

Webb's heart skipped a beat. Sundown was a true rider and she'd be able to get back to Glorian in no time. He, on the other hand, was less than capable on horseback.

"Okay, both of you listen to me," their uncle began. "Wrap your arms tightly around your Muradians and..."

Webb watched his uncle stop cold and go pale. He followed the man's shifting gaze, but could see nothing. Then he realized it wasn't what his uncle had seen, but what he had heard.

It began as a buzz just beyond the horizon, a buzz that Webb knew would soon turn into a distinctive hungry growl. The Whoop-Dingers were coming. His uncle turned his head back around and caught Webb's eyes.

"Both of you wrap your arms as tight as you can around your Muradian's neck and tell it to take you back to Glorian. Kick solidly with both heels and hang on. They will race you back. I'll be right behind you."

"What are you going to do, Unky?" asked Sundown, panicked.

"That doesn't concern you. Just move!" he shouted.

"Uncle Mike-" protested Webb.

"*Move now!*"

Sundown reacted first, hugging PJ tightly and then whispering, "Hurry, to Glorian," in the Muradian's ear. She dug her heels into PJ's side and was off in a burst of speed. The thrust to a full Muradian gallop caused her stomach to lurch and made her arm joints feel like they had been stretched out of their sockets. At first, she kept her eyes closed tight as the wind shot passed her. She could hear the thunder crashing, and she could imagine the splinters of lightning that she knew must be there. Then, whether it was curiosity or something else, she opened her eyes and saw what made her momentarily forget the horrors that were chasing her.

They were flying. She knew it had to be an illusion, but there was no other way to describe it. The hills and plains were rolling by them in a smooth, seamless blur, as if on the rails of a roller coaster. She could not feel nor hear a single hoof beat as they hurtled forward; the transition from hills to plains was so gentle and serene that it seemed impossible that PJ's hooves were actually touching the ground. By resting her chin upon PJ's mane and listening to the wind as it whipped through her hair, she could convince herself, albeit briefly, that they were in flight.

Webb had watched his sister disappear into the distance which took only seconds. It was his turn to flee.

"Go, Webb!" he implored, this time without anger, a flicker of lightning highlighting the anxiety in his face. "I know what I'm doing."

Webb reluctantly wrapped his arms around his Muradian. "To Glorian," he said while kicking its sides. The horse burst forward without hesitation. Clutching the horse as tightly as he could with both his arms, he carefully turned his head around and watched his uncle's statuesque form recede into the distance.

Suddenly an explosion erupted from behind him. It wasn't thunder, but something resonating from the ground. Webb's instinct was to stop his Muradian and return for his uncle, but he knew that would be futile. He clutched the creature's neck as he fought back tears of frustration, anger and complete helplessness. He'd lost his uncle once already. He wasn't ready to do it again.

Glorian glinted conspicuously white in the distance, a welcome sight to both Webb and Sundown's terrified spirits. Sundown had unconsciously tightened her legs on PJ's sides in anxiety when she'd first seen the fortress, slowing PJ down momentarily and enabling Webb to catch up with her. From that point on, they'd rode together.

Webb kept turning his head around, looking for signs of the Whoop-Dingers. He couldn't see them, but he knew they were closing. His uncle couldn't have stopped all of them. He clenched his jaw, stifling the fury that was raging in his heart. In his peripheral vision, he could see his sister looking at him, no doubt desiring some answer as to where "Unky" was, but he wouldn't allow himself to look at her.

Webb felt a small splash of water followed by another and then another. In a matter of moments, their trek to Glorian was encumbered with the downpour of a cold rain. It wasn't a heavy rain, but the speeds at which the Muradians were racing made the water feel like sharp ice chips stinging his face and arms. Thankfully, they were closing upon the castle fast.

They plunged down a small hill and galloped single file, PJ in the lead, towards an entranceway that had suddenly appeared in the outer walls of the fortress. Outlined within the portal, Webb could make out three figures in the forefront and a hoard of others mulling behind them.

The Muradians halted before the entry and leaned forward, gently allowing the siblings to dismount. Both horses then reared back up and bolted out into the darkness at a steady gallop.

"PJ, come back," Sundown shouted and began to take after him.

"It's okay, Sundown," shouted Raven, latching onto Sundown's arm. "The Whoop-Dingers cannot harm them. They are impervious to their evil. Don't worry."

"However, not all of us are as fortunate as the Muradians. *We* are susceptible to them and your impetuousness almost cost you your lives—and still might, if we don't get back inside," hissed a new voice.

It had come from a man with long dark hair in a dark trench coat. His face seemed to be set in a permanent scowl, made even more intimidating by the ominous scar that ran down the right side of his face from the crest of his scalp to his prominent sculpted jaw line.

"But my uncle is still out there," Webb protested.

"Well then, your recklessness has already cost us," he replied.

"Hold off, Kane," came the soft voice of Mathias.

The unpleasant man turned, his scarred face set in anger.

"We still have a bit of time," Mathias replied.

"It's my fault, Mathias," cried Webb. "Sundown and I were near the Requiem and Uncle Mike came and got us. Six o'clock snuck up on us. Honestly! Uncle Mike sent us back and he stayed behind to fight off the Whoop-Dingers."

"I am aware of what happened and nobody blames you," soothed Mathias, his hands resting on Webb's damp shoulders. "Your uncle took the correct course of action."

"But he's no match for all those things. Someone needs to go back and get him," Webb pleaded.

"Yes, that's a *very* wise idea," droned Kane sarcastically under his breath.

Mathias shot him a disapproving glance and then focused on Webb's anguished face. "Michael doesn't have to stop them, Webb. He just needed to delay them."

"What about the storm? It came out of nowhere. Won't that slow him down?" asked Sundown, rushing up next to her brother.

"The storm is merely a way for the Dark Lands to purge certain imbalances, whatever they may be," Mathias explained. "It is inconsequential to your uncle's flight. Water is only water."

As if on cue, there was a flash of lightning revealing a lone rider on the horizon, quickly closing upon Glorian. Webb and Sundown both started forward, but were grabbed and held fast by Mathias, who was surprisingly strong for his thin and aged appearance. Webb could just make out his uncle's fearful face as he kicked his heels and pushed his Muradian to its limits. Webb looked beyond him and saw what made his heart almost stop—a swarm of Whoop-Dingers. Their transparent tissues glistened even more wetly under the lightning and rain; the telltale growls growing closer and closer.

"*Move it, Michael,*" Webb thought he heard Kane hiss under his breath, but he couldn't be sure through the howling rain and clapping thunder.

Suddenly, to everyone's relief, the Muradian was at the entrance, panting and snorting with exertion. Uncle Michael, impaired leg and all, leapt off the heaving animal and scrambled inside clumsily.

"DO IT!" he screamed breathlessly to Kane.

Kane quickly brushed everyone back as he slammed the huge double wooden doors shut with a quick motion of his hand. They locked in place with a damp dull thud. He then grabbed the key that Webb had seen his uncle use the night before and jammed it in the enormous keyhole. Kane cranked the key and the familiar low rumble began to reverberate in the halls and passageways throughout Glorian and then, for the briefest of moments, all was quiet. Everyone perked their ears, their breathing momentarily stilled, waiting for the inevitable cacophony of sounds that would soon come.

Moments later they heard it.

Shrill cries and outraged screams suddenly tore through the fortress, causing several of the onlookers to involuntarily step back in disquiet. The walls shook and the screams were full of an anger that Webb hadn't heard the night before, the nature of the cries more violent and frustrated from having just barely lost their quarry. He felt arms encircle him and found Sundown pressed against him, shivering. He returned her embrace, putting his hands over her ears as she grimaced from the noise.

Webb looked instinctively over to Mathias who was nodding his head almost imperceptibly. He caught Webb's glance and looked back towards him. "So close and yet so far," he commented before nodding a goodnight and heading back to his chambers.

Webb then turned to find Kane gazing upon them. Moreover, he seemed to be looking directly at Sundown, his face caught somewhere between shock and sorrow. A moment later when Kane caught sight of Webb staring at him, he turned briskly and left, his long coat flapping behind him with each step.

Sundown lifted her head and looked behind her. Lying against the wall was the rain-soaked figure of Uncle Mike, his cane lying limply in his left hand. His eyes, previously wide with adrenaline, were now lulling. Sundown moved from Webb to her uncle and held him tightly.

"I was so worried," she sniffed, burying her face into his shoulder.

"Shhhhh," he whispered.

Michael stroked the girl's hair comfortingly and Webb thought he saw Sundown's shoulders heave momentarily in evidence of a sob, but the shoulders quickly settled as she recomposed herself.

Webb noticed Raven and about ten other Glorians still milling around the scene, alternating their glances between Sundown, himself and the great door. He offered a half-hearted smile in their direction, one that was part salutation, part apology. Most of them appeared to be in their thirties save for a younger man in the forefront, a blonde who, by Webb's estimate, was close to his own age.

The young man smiled and nodded towards Webb before filing out along with everyone else. Soon, all that remained in the entry chamber were Webb, Raven, Sundown and Uncle Mike.

Sundown was still sitting by her uncle, silently taking in the awful sounds that were emanating from outside. Webb was about to walk over and check on her when Raven interceded and knelt down beside his sister.

"Let's go eat. You need a break after all that," she said, offering her hand. Sundown accepted it and they quickly disappeared down the hallway.

Webb settled down next to his uncle, unsure as to what he should say. Everything seemed awkward now. Thankfully, he didn't have to be the one to break the silence.

"That was fun wasn't it?" his uncle said humorously.

"I'm really sorry, Uncle Mike," Webb apologized, heavy-hearted.

"What for? You did nothing wrong."

Webb looked at him incredulously. "Nothing wrong? Just a few seconds here or there and it would have been a disaster!"

"But it wasn't a disaster, was it? Worst case, you learned a lesson."

"It's lucky though. Your Muradian must have been a tad faster than ours to get here as quickly as you did," said Webb.

"No, the Muradians are all consistent. None faster. None slower."

"Then how did you get back here without those creatures catching you? They were almost on you when I left."

"It's just a matter of slowing them down, son. You'll learn soon enough." He then winked at Webb, bringing a smile of relief to his nephew's face.

For the remainder of the hour, they rested against the wall and listened as the Dark Man's manifestations flailed themselves mercilessly against the castle walls. Michael remained very calm throughout the ordeal while Webb himself jumped at the more intense crashes from the assault. He wondered how long it would take for him to get used to the noise.

When the attacks finally stopped and the seven-o'clock hour rang true, Uncle Mike limped to the keyhole and wrenched the key. The usual rumbling vibrations ran throughout the walls. Webb made a mental note to later ask what the key business was all about. Once the quaking had fully stopped, his uncle turned to face him.

"I want to show you something," he said as he pushed the entryway open.

Webb jumped forward in a start, "Uncle Mike, no! Those things could still be out there!"

"Webb, calm down. They're gone," he reassured him. "Now, step outside with me for just a minute. You should see something here."

Webb couldn't understand what there was to see out there. He knew that by day there nothing to look at beyond the walls but endless green grass and darkened storm clouds; he couldn't imagine what there would be to see in the pitch dark of night. Nevertheless, he nervously followed his uncle outside, the fresh smell of the storm still drifting in the air, reminding Webb of the scent of autumn rains back home. His footfalls did not squelch as much on the ground as he had anticipated. The grass had done a good job of absorbing all the water.

When they were both several steps from the entrance, which was much too far away for Webb's comfort, his uncle stopped and motioned to him. "Now, if you're done staring at the ground, look up."

Webb obliged and his expression changed instantly.

Surrounding him in the blackened skies were stars, closer and brighter than any he'd ever encountered even on the clearest nights back home. Not only that; there were also full winding galaxies, and clusters of stars and planets. Before him was a dazzling cornucopia of golds, blues, greens, every color that could be imagined and some that could not, all swirled into sparkling perfection. On the horizon he could make out an aqua blue planet, similar to Earth, but void of any land masses and much more pristine in color. Everywhere he looked, his field of vision was saturated with awing beauty. This was why Mathias had told him he should come out to see the sky at night.

The stars twinkled their luminance from afar; the planets ebbed and flowed around these fiery giants while the galaxies churned their never-ending glitter of colors into perfect spirals. It was almost more than he could accept. He tried to mouth his feelings, but nothing would come.

"Glad you came outside now?" asked Uncle Mike as he watched the boy's face in amusement.

Webb offered something of a vague nod.

"I like to come out here at night," he continued. "Reminds me that for everything bad, there is something just as good out there, if not better."

"So beautiful, so perfect," Webb managed to slur out under his breath. He had no idea how long he stood there gazing into the heavens. When he emerged out of his daze, he found himself alone on the grounds, his uncle having left him to his own whiles. Webb blinked his eyes a few times and then walked back inside, taking one last look behind him before shutting the doors.

Webb found his room shortly thereafter, happy that he was getting the hang of finding what he needed in Glorian. He knew he should probably eat, but the idea of a good night's sleep sounded much more appealing to him at the moment. The whole fiasco with the Requiem and six o'clock had worn him out. He figured that he would just eat a larger breakfast in the morning to make up for it.

Upon opening the door to his room he was greeted by a familiar purring sound. Lying luxuriously across his bed was Gustafson, eyes staring lazily at him. Webb threw his damp coat onto his desk chair and gauged the big cat amusingly.

"Haven't seen you all day. Where you been?"

Gustafson let out a short meow in response.

"Oh," answered Webb, pretending to understand for the sake of conversation. "So you thought you'd just let yourself in?"

Webb wondered briefly how Gustafson managed to get into his room with no thumbs to turn the doorknob. Oh well, Mathias had said Gustafson's kind could traverse worlds, so what was a little wooden door to creature like that? In any case, the big cat's presence made him feel a little more secure. Webb rubbed the feline's furry ear affectionately, remembering how Gustafson had rescued him and his sister when they'd first arrived.

"Gustafson, my friend, I know you want to be pet, but I'm exhausted. I'm going to sleep, so goodnight to you," Webb chimed as he shut his lights out and crawled into bed, the soft covers making his eyelids very heavy.

Within minutes, Webb was blissfully sound asleep with Gustafson snuggled warmly by his side.

CHAPTER ELEVEN

RUDE AWAKENING

Webb woke to the rich smell of oatmeal. He followed the smell to his desk where a bowl of hot steamy oatmeal awaited him. Cascaded atop the cereal was brown sugar and raisins, just the right amount, and completing the picture was a large glass of milk, glistening droplets of condensation outlining the glass. Webb sighed contently.

He stepped out of bed, ignoring Gustafson's reproachful look. To a Felix, the thought of waking up before noon was rather egregious.

Gustafson's gawking notwithstanding, Webb took a deep whiff of the oatmeal and sat down at his desk. He dug into the bowl and consumed an enormous helping. It was just as delicious as he'd imagined. For the briefest of moments he was back home and it was Saturday morning. His mom would be knocking on his door any minute to make sure he was up and getting ready to go to work. He could feel the cold winds of October and smell the fireplaces that were already starting to burn.

He drank some milk and then turned his attention to the picture frame on the far right of his desk. There, in a black and white photograph, stood his mom and dad lovingly embracing Sundown and himself. In the background, the cresting waves of Corpus Christi could just be seen. All four of them had smiles on their faces, the warm, genuine smiles of a loving family. This photograph had been taken just a few years back while they had been on their annual family vacation at the beach. Webb took his finger and gently moved it over the images of his mom and dad. He wondered about his parents and what they were doing, how they were feeling—their two children, their *only* two children, taken from them. It made him hurt.

He absently took another bite of his oatmeal and leaned back in his chair, its leather making a squeaky stretching sound against his bare legs. Seventeen years old and life was over before it had really begun. He hadn't even gotten to graduate from high school or get a real job.

Webb looked away from the picture and took another bite of his oatmeal, the brown sugar melting in his mouth and stickily coating his throat which was tightening with emotion. He washed it all down with another gulp of cold milk. His eyes caught another glimpse of the photograph before he tore his gaze away, blinking rapidly to fight back the images and welling sadness.

When the food was finished, he stood from his chair and went to dress. He saw that Gustafson was still on his bed, curled in a tight circle with his tail over his face, asleep.

"Tough life you got there, Gus," muttered Webb as he went to his closet and pulled out some jeans and another t-shirt. Looking at Gustafson, Webb was still amazed at the size of the cat. He was comparable to a very large dog, but otherwise so feline. The Felidaes were about as bizarre as anything else he had encountered in the Dark Lands, but at least he knew Gustafson was on his side.

He dressed and then walked over to his bed and looked down upon the sleeping Felix. Webb scratched the cat's head, receiving a groggy purr in return. Suddenly, there were three short raps at his door.

Webb anticipated finding either Mathias or Sundown on the other side. Waiting there instead was someone else.

CHAPTER TWELVE

CONTROLLED ANGER

"Good morning, Webb," came Kane's clipped, disingenuous greeting.

Webb just stared back, his eyes blinking wildly. "Where's Mathias?"

Kane sneered, the scar on his face skewing awkwardly. "Mathias has many things to do and Glorian cannot afford him playing nurse mate to you at every waking hour," he replied while brushing past.

Webb watched as Kane scornfully appraised every inch of his room. When he was done he turned back around to Webb. "Are you ready?" he asked, the less than friendly smirk making its return.

"Ready for what?" asked Webb, his stomach involuntarily knotting.

"Didn't Mathias tell you about today?" he asked impatiently.

"He said I'd learn about my gift."

"Exactly. Now, shall we go?" replied Kane, motioning to the door.

"Sure." Webb hastily grabbed his jacket and followed Kane out of the room. He didn't like this at all. Mathias was supposed to be his mentor or counselor or whatever, not this jerk with the colossal personality defect. How did he get stuck with scarface?

Kane walked very quickly, making it difficult for Webb to keep up with him. The man's motions were so precise and deliberate that Webb thought he must have been in the military back in the living world.

"So, uh, Mathias couldn't make it today?"

"He asked that I instruct you on this matter," answered Kane dryly.

"So, you're a teacher?" he continued, trying to ferret out what Kane's position was.

The question stopped Kane immediately. He gave Webb another unpleasant glower before continuing down the hallway. "This is not a *school*, Webb. I am not some babysitter for impetuous children. I serve on the Glorian Council just as Mathias does. *That* is who I am. Any more questions?" he replied with growing impatience.

Webb didn't reply. He just continued briskly marching beside Kane, not bothering to hide the sullen look that was now spreading across his own face.

The silence between the two continued as they navigated the hallway, Kane's dogged stride making the other Glorians en route to breakfast have to dodge out of the way for fear of being trampled. Webb thought he saw a few sympathetic looks directed his way as they passed.

Soon they'd left everyone behind and were heading towards an area of Glorian Webb was almost certain he'd never seen before. Direction was a somewhat relative thing in the Dark Lands anyway, but he'd always had the feeling he'd been on the east side of Glorian and now he and Kane were taking a more western course.

They were closing fast upon a set of monstrous doors for which Kane was making no signs of slowing down nor even extending his hands in order to push them open. Webb began to fall back, not wanting to crash face first into the doors like Kane seemed intent on doing.

Suddenly, Kane made the briefest swipe with his left hand and the mammoth doors flung outward, almost tearing themselves off the hinges of the walls as they did so. Kane passed through them quickly, Webb just making it through before the doors slammed back into place.

"Keep up," called Kane over his shoulder.

Webb looked back at the doors as they settled in place. He had to admit that was one of the most awesome things he'd ever seen. He wanted to ask

Kane exactly how he had done it, but knew he'd probably just get another sneer.

The pair walked hundreds of yards out from Glorian, Kane saying nothing and Webb asking nothing all the while. They started up a steep incline and when they'd reached the top Webb saw it leveled off to a plateau that offered an intense panoramic view. There were still the same grays, blacks and greens surrounding him, but now Webb could make out a few landmarks he had not noticed before: a clear blue lake that he perceived as south of the Glorian compound and a tortuous river that snaked towards it. A slight gust of wind whispered by, chilling him. He turned back around and found Kane staring at him, but this time the eye contact did not seem caustic; it was more like an appraisal.

"I brought you up here, Webb, so that you could better appreciate your position. To make you realize that this is not a game. This is not a place to have fun," Kane growled. "For better or worse, you are part of the Dark Lands now. An actual part of it, just like the skies, the grass, or Glorian itself."

Webb nodded.

"Then you'll appreciate that your impetuousness, which was very prominently on display last night, will not be tolerated here."

"That's like the third time you've used 'impetuous' to describe me," answered Webb tiredly.

"Would you like me to do it a fourth time? Or shall we do something more productive with what time has been allotted to us?"

Webb bit his lip.

"Good. Now, I don't have Mathias' tolerance for your youthful enthusiasm. In fact, I find it a liability which puts us all in danger. Alas, you are here and will be trained accordingly," spoke Kane in his clipped manner. "Now, today, you are going to learn about your 'gift'—the one thing you possess that will enable you to fight off and destroy the Vindicadives."

"I guess plain old fighting doesn't work, huh?" Webb added sarcastically, rolling his eyes Kane's way.

A dark smile slid up the good side of Kane's face. "Yes, 'plain old fighting' might do if nothing else were available. Of course then, you might as well just give yourself to the Vindicadives. Let them turn you into a Whoop-Dinger, or better yet, a Menschenklaus. I understand the process is much more terrifying and the existence even worse."

"I didn't mean-" Webb started defensively.

"You'll soon find there is quite a bit you don't know here, Mr. Thompson," interrupted Kane with a biting glare. "What I am talking about is the ability to literally stop and/or destroy masses of Vindicadives, not just a chance one or two with your mere fists."

I can fight off and destroy masses of Vindicadives? Webb fought off the urge to smile, but he was suddenly feeling very tough, not as helpless as before.

"Everyone here has a gift. It is my task to find yours. It will then be *your* task to *cultivate* it," Kane said pointedly.

"By myself?"

"No, Webb," sighed Kane. "You will have help: training." He paused momentarily, giving Webb a rather disquieting look that seemed to be Kane's attempt at inviting another question, though it actually dissuaded Webb from doing that very thing. "Now, have you learned about your existence here?"

"I'm... a reflection?" Webb answered hesitantly.

Kane nodded. "And therefore, your gift is a further reflection of what you possessed in the living world, part of your *essence*."

Webb skewed his head confusingly. He didn't understand what "essence" Kane was referring to.

"A reflection of your personality," Kane offered frustratingly. "Your personality is a manifestation of who you really are and that is what your gift draws upon."

He paused and reached into the pocket of his dark trench coat, pulling from it a handful of marbles, translucent and blood-red in color. He then casually cast them on the ground in front of him, their red color shining in the emerald green grass.

"Your rather... *forceful* personality," spoke Kane haltingly, "leads me to believe that you will follow in your uncle's footsteps. He is what is known in the Dark Lands as a *Disperser*."

"And what's that?" Webb asked.

"In simple terms, one who possesses the ability to repel something, practically anything. Let me show you." He inclined his hand towards the scattered marbles and made a simple brushing gesture.

The marbles erupted off the ground and rolled forward, coming to a stop just a few feet away. Webb stared, eyes widened, at Kane. "You did the same thing a few minutes ago to the door," he said, pointing back to Glorian in astonishment.

"So, you *were* paying attention," scoffed Kane.

Webb rolled his eyes. "Well, it was kind of hard to ignore."

"In time, you'll hone your ability and be able to do the same. From the most subtle of sensations," announced Kane, making a circular motion in the air with his hand that caused a breeze to tickle past Webb's cheek. "To the most volatile," he continued, thrusting his arm forward, his hand rigidly perpendicular to the ground. The earth before them abruptly exploded in a flurry of dirt and grass.

Webb shook the debris off his clothes as he looked into the enormous rift that now existed where grass and earth had been. "I'll be able to do that?" he asked wide-eyed.

"And more, if you don't slack in your training," Kane replied, measuring the boy's reaction while the ground before them began to heal itself, earth and grass miraculously rejuvenating where the chasm had been. "Now, *you* try," Kane said sternly.

"Me? But you said in time..."

"And that time is *now*."

Webb opened his mouth to begin to protest, but could not successfully articulate an intelligent argument. Instead, he just shrugged his shoulders in surrender. "Whatever. What do I do?" he asked resignedly.

Kane gritted his teeth at the boy's insolence. "The first step to successfully mastering anything is focus. F-O-C-U-S. Something *you* seem to lack."

"Fine, I'm focused," Webb fired back. "Teach me."

Kane reached down and grabbed one of the marbles. He picked it up and held it at eye level, rolling it between thumb and forefinger. "Point your finger at this marble and knock it from my grasp."

Webb swallowed and extended his index finger directly at the red marble, focusing on blasting it free. When nothing happened, he began vigorously jousting his finger back and forth in the air. But still, nothing happened.

"And you said you were focused," sighed Kane.

"You're holding it too tight," Webb retorted.

Aggravated, Kane grabbed Webb's hand and shoved the marble into his palm. "Bury it as tight as you possibly can in your fist," he barked.

Webb did as he was told, looking bitingly at Kane in the process. "Ready?"

Webb gave a terse nod.

Kane curtly snapped his index finger at Webb's fist, sending the marble spiraling free from his grasp.

"Ouch!" Webb hissed, rubbing his raw palm.

"Now, shall we try it again or do you need time for another excuse, boy?"

Webb picked up another of the marbles from the ground and tossed it at Kane. "Hold it up," he demanded.

Kane complied and Webb again forcefully pointed his finger at the marble, his head spinning with embarrassment and anger. But again, nothing happened.

"It requires focus, Webb. Your thoughts need to be solely on removing this marble from my fingers. Your mind cannot be drifting to a thousand different places like some inattentive child."

Webb shook with anger as he continued to point his finger futilely at the marble, his face turning red.

"FOCUS, boy!" Kane snarled. "You are never going to protect yourself, much less anyone else here, without focus. Not that protection has ever been one of your strong suits. You obviously weren't able to protect your *sister* in the living world, or she wouldn't be here with you now. Would she?"

Webb felt his entire body shriek with fury. How dare Kane accuse him of not being able to protect Sundown. Who was he to make such a judgment? He didn't know him, didn't know him in the least. He didn't know how they died. Nobody did. The blood boiling in his ears,

Webb's thoughts converged directly on one mental image: *knocking that smug look off of Kane's face.* Emulating what he'd seen Kane do moments before, Webb positioned his hand perpendicular to the ground and rifled it forward in Kane's direction.

For a split second, it seemed to Webb that everything had gone silent. Nothing moved, save for what appeared to be apparition-like waves emanating from his hand, but then everything exploded forth in a violent serenade of sound. The last thing Webb saw were Kane's eyes growing wide before the man was literally blown backwards off of the plateau. The booming echo of the explosion radiated out over the horizon.

Webb dropped to his knees, suddenly feeling spent. Sweat began to cascade down his brow. For a moment he felt lost, not knowing where he was or why he was there, but it all came back to him in a panic. He looked to where Kane had been standing and nothing was there but strewn dirt and a lone red marble shining in the grass.

"Oh no," he mouthed.

Through the breeze, Webb could make out the sound of uneven footfalls just beyond the plateau. They grew louder in approach. He looked to the plateau's edge and saw nothing. Then, a crown of dark hair broke the green of the plain, followed by Kane's dark scowl, his figure growing more fearsome and ominous as he limped back up the steep hill. Webb couldn't rise. He just sat there, expecting some form of painful retribution.

Kane reached the top and began to methodically stagger towards Webb, every step resounding with controlled anger. When he was about five feet from the boy, he stopped and stared unflinchingly upon him.

"Just as I thought," he hissed. "Your gift resonates from your inner anger. And there is no place for that within Glorian."

"What?" Webb's eyes widened. Was he being removed from Glorian?

"Your anger, you tap into it too easily. It makes you reckless. What's more, it makes you *dangerous*."

"So what do you want me to do about it?"

"Learn," replied Kane, turning back towards the fortress. "Today's lesson is over."

For a time, Webb just sat there alone on the plateau, morose and angry, while the winds whipped at his hair. How was he expected to learn anything with everyone replying in riddles or, in Kane's case, practically not replying at all? And if scarface was supposed to be the one to teach him how to be a Disperser, then he might as well just lock himself up in his room and ride out his stay in the Dark Lands as a hermit. They had barely even begun their lesson together, and he already felt like he had failed some kind of test.

Webb looked back to the castle and saw that Kane had already disappeared inside without him. Once again, he was alone.

─── CHAPTER THIRTEEN ───

THE RECLAIMER'S TALE

Raven knocked on Sundown's door and was immediately received with a sweet chirp "come in." Opening the door, she was greeted by the splash and flare of a teenage girl's room, or at least what Raven construed as one. It had been so long since she'd been privy to the styles of the living world, much less that of a modern teenager, that she just assumed this was otherworld normalcy.

The walls were an electric red and blue splayed with posters of various male "heartthrobs" and female "divas," two terms that Raven had been familiarized with during her initial sessions with Sundown. Propped on a bed overflowing with a variety of stuffed animals, was her young charge, engaged in reading some glossy booklet that Raven couldn't identify.

"Hi Raven," greeted Sundown, setting the magazine aside. "I am so excited about today!" It was the third time she'd told Raven as much in the matter of an hour—twice at breakfast and once now.

Raven hesitantly returned the smile and sat down on the edge of Sundown's bed, a few of the stuffed "friends" falling to the floor as she did so. She took a deep breath, her face still not betraying the worries and concerns that were coursing through her.

"I think that part of your excitement stems from you having a good idea as to what your gift is. You may not know what it is called, but you know what you can do," said Raven, looking deep into Sundown's questioning brown eyes.

The girl sat up and crossed her legs casually. "Okay, I'm game," she replied. "But, what're you talking about?"

Raven paused. Initially, she had thought it best to engage Sundown in some neutral environment, like in one of the many classrooms or offices scattered throughout Glorian, but her intuition had suggested that this conversation be held in an environment where Sundown would feel more secure, some place where she wouldn't feel so vulnerable. Despite her long separation from the living world, Raven still remembered that a girl's room was the place where she would share her deepest secrets. So that was where she had sent Sundown after breakfast while she, in turn, had paced the hallways debating how to best approach the subject of Sundown's gift.

"Why don't you tell me what happened out there, on the deep moors when you and Webb first arrived."

Sundown furrowed her brow. "I've told you before. We were chased down by those Whoop-Dinger things and then Gustafson saved us."

"Is that it?" Raven pressed.

Sundown shrugged uncertainly. "I guess so. That's how Webb would probably describe it."

"No, Sundown," whispered Raven. "Tell me what *you* remember— not what Webb said happened."

Sundown gasped. "You *know*?" Tears began to spill from her eyes, the dichotomy of terrible events no longer seeming so absurd to her.

"Yes, I know," soothed Raven. "Now, why don't you start at the beginning?"

Sundown took a deep breath and the words began to flow shakily, but unbridled.

"Where are Mom and Dad, Webb? Where are they, Webb? Where are they!?" Sundown heard herself screaming hysterically, her voice carrying as a shrill echo across the plains.

"I don't know!" Webb replied. "I don't know. But we're not going to find them by waiting here."

Sundown felt completely overcome with fear. She began to sob uncontrollably, her cries encompassing and clouding everything in her mind.

She felt Webb hug her and begin whispering assurances of well-being. For that moment, the embrace was the only thing that had meaning to Sundown and she swam in it for as long as she could. It was very surreal to her; she could hear herself wailing, but she seemed removed from it, more attuned to her brother's embrace and words of comfort.

Then, she became one again and looked up to see a horror she could never have known existed. Rushing towards her and Webb at a speed that seemed impossible were these translucent creatures, almost like giant blobs of dirty water. They were shrieking insanely, sounds that Sundown had never heard before nor did she ever want to hear again. The shrieks were echoing everywhere, rasping at her eardrums, eating away at everything. Sundown initially couldn't understand how these horrors had snuck upon them until she realized that her cries had monopolized all sound in their ears up until that point, giving the creatures the acoustic camouflage they'd needed.

She spun Webb around, sheer terror robbing her of the ability to scream or even speak. From that point, everything seemed to move in slow motion.

Webb pushed Sundown away, ordering her to run, but she was too frightened to do anything but fall limply to the ground. Through tear-engorged eyes, she watched as her brother attempted to tackle the nearest creature and wrestle it to the ground. Instead he fell right through it, his face grimacing in pain.

Webb rolled over, his expression changing from one of pain to one of absolute revulsion as the creature he had tried to stop began to metamorphose into a banshee-like monster. It drew close to Webb, its mouth opening with a sickening gasp, before quickly pulling him into its hollow wet innards.

Sundown began to shake as Webb struggled within the watery phantasm, his mouth opening and closing in muffled screaming while his fists and feet kicked in every direction, trying to find a way out.

Webb then let loose a final gurgle before his features suddenly began to melt together, the colors of his body spilling out with his innards and swirling around him like macabre paint in a churning pool of turpentine.

She cupped her hands over her ears, trying to shut out the horrific sounds that her imagination conjured up as she watched her brother die. She mouthed words of sorrow and apology, wishing more than anything that she hadn't been so hysterical before, that she'd kept it together enough so that they would have had more warning of these monsters' approach. If she hadn't broken down and distracted Webb, maybe then they would have had a chance to escape.

The once translucent creature, now awash in her brother's remains, suddenly vomited out another creature similar to it, but Sundown knew that this was not just another monster. This one had once been her brother. She then, finally found her scream.

Sundown had never wailed in such a way. All of her love for Webb and her disgust at the horror around her contained in one primordial cry. And then everything literally stopped.

There was nothing. No movement. No sound. It was like pausing a movie, viewing a still picture within a vacuum.

Sundown felt overcome with the surreal feeling of transcendentalism. Everything around her started to move backwards, not away from her, but backwards as if life itself was rewinding. She watched in muted awe as her brother's form materialized once again inside the creature and then was repelled out of its mouth and onto the grass. Webb then made a backwards leap from the ground and through the monster. Then, she herself began to drift back towards her brother as the translucent creatures receded. Everything was slowly materializing to the way it had been before the attack and Sundown knew that she was the cause of it. She was controlling it. Her wish to be able to correct her wrongs was manifesting itself before her. Then, without warning, she was standing in real time before her brother on the plains of the Dark Lands, the events of the past few minutes nothing more than a vivid nightmare.

Sundown sat on her bed, her tear-soaked eyes staring into her quilted duvet. "And so there we were, back to where it had all started, before the creatures got there. This time I didn't freak out," she sniffed. "This time, I held my ground. I just crossed my arms and planted myself there. I must have looked like quite the priss," she weakly laughed, another tear drifting down her cheek. "I waited until we could hear the sounds of the Whoop-Dingers. I wanted Webb to realize the danger. I mean I couldn't just *tell* him what had happened. He wouldn't…"

"Believe you?" Raven offered, brushing Sundown's tears away.

Sundown nodded.

"But now you know it was real," affirmed Raven.

Sundown offered a half-hearted smile and wiped her nose. "Yeah, I'd say so."

"You've got a great gift, my angel, perhaps the greatest in the Dark Lands."

"What's it called?"

"We call it being a *Reclaimer*," answered Raven. "A Reclaimer has the ability to turn back time, to rewind it and start over from a certain point."

"That's exactly what I did," Sundown exclaimed, traces of both nervousness and excitement in her voice. "I went back and changed things. It was like I was given a second chance, allowed to change things for the better."

"That's what we do," spoke Raven stoically. "Or at least, that is what we try to do."

"We? You're a Reclaimer too?" asked Sundown, her eyes lighting up.

"Yes, I am. That is why I was matched with you as your counselor."

"How many more of us are there?"

"Very few. It is a rare gift, given only to the purest of souls and, moreover, given only to women."

Sundown's eyes stared off into space for a moment, her mind rife with questions. "How far back can we go? I mean, are there limits?"

"No one really knows the limits because no one can prove or disprove a Reclaimer's account."

"What do you mean no one can prove or disprove? I just told you what I did. Webb and I are both still here because of it. Isn't that proof enough?"

"I have no proof you did anything. Only your word—not that I don't trust you," she added.

"My word? But didn't you…" Sundown faltered. She now understood what Raven was saying. The first reality, where Webb had been destroyed and transformed by the Whoop-Dinger, had been overwritten by the second reality that she had initiated. The first reality had therefore never been experienced by anyone aside from herself. For all intents and purposes, it had never happened.

"So, I'm the only one who remembers…"

"Yes. When you step back in time, you are the only one who will ever remember the alternate reality. It will be as clear to you as any of your memories, but no one else will ever have a recollection of it. To them, it never happened." Raven looked away and then added, almost absently, "…And who's to say it didn't?"

Sundown looked contemplatively at Raven's abrupt change in tone, but said nothing of it.

"Death can be reversed. Love can be erased," Raven continued. "New things can be torn asunder; old things can be mended."

"Amazing," Sundown said.

Raven nodded somberly.

"But how did you know I was a Reclaimer?"

"I've been one long enough to know the look of a Reclaimer, the aura that settles upon them."

"You almost sound like it's a bad thing," said Sundown, no longer able to ignore Raven's sullen disposition.

The woman shifted uncomfortably. She didn't want to sour her young charge, but Sundown needed to be aware that everything had a consequence. "There are times, dear, when our gift isn't necessarily… a blessing."

"How? How can changing what went wrong ever be bad?"

Raven smiled sadly. "You are so innocent still, so sweet, so truly pure."

Sundown smiled back doubtfully, unsure if she had just received a compliment or not.

"I am saturated with memories of horrors I've had to erase, of emotions that can never be requited, of people who no longer exist, and I have not a soul to confide in," continued Raven, focusing on keeping her voice cool and even. "Do you see the difficulties inherent in what I am describing?"

Sundown looked introspective, but Raven could see that she did not understand.

"Did you have a best friend back in the living world, Sunny?" asked Raven, opting for a different tact.

"Yes. Her name is Lauren," answered Sundown, reflecting on slumber parties and their long phone conversations about boys and fashion.

"How would you feel if suddenly, from Lauren's perspective, your whole history together was erased? To you, nothing had changed, but to her, it had never happened. For the rest of your days, you'd have memories and feelings for a relationship that only *you* remembered. Imagine how sad that would be."

Sundown's eyes appeared to glaze over at the solemn thought. "...I think I understand," she replied hesitantly.

Raven reached over and grabbed both of her arms tightly. "That is why you must be so *careful*, Sundown. If you overuse your gift, you could be forever plagued with countless emotions and experiences that aren't rooted in anything real around you." Raven leaned in closer, barely speaking above a whisper. "You have a great gift. Don't let what I am sharing with you ever dissuade you of that. But you need to learn how to utilize it and temper it. You control it; don't let it control you."

"It's *my* gift. How can it control me?"

"The omnipotence of it all, the feeling that you can control everything can become addictive. ...Sometimes you change things that should not be changed."

Raven's last words came out like verbalized ice, chilling Sundown's spine. She looked back into Raven's dark eyes and was haunted by the pain she saw hiding behind the shining onyx irises. "What happened to you, Raven? What did you do?"

Raven pulled back. For a moment, she actually thought about reclaiming their conversation, but the better part of prudence took over and she realized how ludicrous that was.

"Some other time," offered Raven dismissively.

Sundown desperately wanted to press the matter further, but knew better than to dig into a woman's personal business when she was not wanted. "So what do we do now?" she asked, changing the subject.

"Follow me." Raven got up off Sundown's bed and headed out the door feeling slightly embarrassed. She had been so absorbed in making sure that Sundown appreciated both sides of her gift that she'd inadvertently opened herself up. But it had been necessary. Raven wasn't going to have Sundown be afflicted with the same kinds of scars she herself had endured for so long. The two left the room quietly, Raven standing tall and rigid under a confident façade.

"Okay," announced Raven when she and Sundown were but a few feet from Sundown's bedroom door. "I want you to use your gift and take us back, just a few seconds to before we left your room."

Sundown was startled. "What?"

"Take us back."

"But I don't know how."

"Sure you do. You've already done it once before and under much more duress. It's all about focus. Stand here and think about nothing else but stepping back."

"O-okay, I'll try," stammered Sundown, less than sure of herself.

Raven placed a hand on Sundown's shoulder. "Relax."

Sundown nodded and breathed out deeply.

"Now, I am going to tell you a secret. Something I know that I haven't shared with you. After you reclaim a few seconds worth of time, I want you to relay it back to me. That way, I will know for certain that you really did reclaim."

"Okay," answered Sundown nervously.

Raven whispered her secret gently into Sundown's ear, causing the younger girl to burst out giggling.

"Okay, concentrate," smiled Raven.

Sundown looked away from Raven and down the hallway. She felt kind of silly just staring off into nothingness while Raven watched her. She hoped no one else would walk by or else she'd feel *really* foolish.

"Stop feeling so self-conscious," Raven offered, sensing the girl's awkwardness, "and just focus."

Sundown nodded apologetically. She then took another deep breath, clearing her mind and focusing her gaze down the hallway. Then, it started. Everything went silent, the eerie vacuum of reclaiming time once again surrounding her. The familiar transcendental feeling, the same feeling she'd experienced on the moors, enveloped Sundown again as she watched Raven and herself move backwards. It was almost as if she were in a state of duality: one self-watching and manipulating the regression of the time line, the other being manipulated by it. Sundown then focused her desire to moving the time line back to its normal flow and, as if she had flipped a switch, normalcy resumed.

Sundown's skin tingled and she felt herself acclimate with the time continuum, the sound of Raven's voice rising in volume as it moved to the foreground of her consciousness.

"Follow me," she heard Raven say.

"The first boy you ever kissed was Peter O'Brien! When you were twelve years old!" Sundown blurted out.

"What?" asked Raven, turning from the door.

"I just did it. I just reclaimed. You told me to tell you about Peter O'Brien when I'd successfully done it. I-it was our code," Sundown stammered out, her excitement making her shake.

Raven sat back down on the bed and gave Sundown a hug. "You did it!" she exclaimed. "How far back did you go?"

"Just a few seconds. Less than a minute. Nowhere near as long as the other day, but I didn't know what I was doing then," Sundown said excitedly. "I completely controlled this one, from beginning to ending!"

"That's wonderful, Sunny," Raven praised. "Alright, for the rest of the day I want you to practice very subtle step backs. *Subtle*, understand?"

Sundown nodded gleefully, beaming.

"And I want you to practice alone. Here in your room, or the Glorian hallways *only* when no one else is around." Raven's tone was stern, bordering on parental.

"I will. Don't worry," responded Sundown.

But Raven was very worried.

── CHAPTER FOURTEEN ──

IN NEED OF A FRIEND

elf-pity quickly gave way to hot anger as Webb stumbled down the hill en route back to Glorian, a fistful of red marbles spilling from his hand and rolling down the hillside with him. Brushing himself off, he began to curse Kane under his breath, certain that the fall was somehow his fault. What kind of a teacher was scarface going to be anyway if all he did was antagonize him and then storm off when he finally got his comeuppance?

A wry smile crept over Webb's face as he thought back to knocking Kane off of the plateau. Admittedly, he was initially terrified when he realized what he'd done, his first impression being that he'd somehow obliterated the man. Of course, that hadn't been the case and Kane had lived to browbeat him once again. Webb spit a gritty combination of grass and dirt from his mouth as he collected the stray marbles, careful to put them in his jacket pocket before continuing on.

The doors to Glorian seemed to bounce before him with each angry step and soon, he was at the entrance. *Focus.* Webb swept his hand forward, exactly as he'd seen Kane do, anticipating the doors flying open at any second. He was so sure of it that he kept his undaunted pace right up to where he smacked directly into the unflinching wood and spilled backwards onto the ground.

Webb sat up and rubbed his throbbing head, certain there was a rough impression of the door's wood grain branded across it. He then remembered that the doors opened *outward*, not inward. Instead of trying to open them, he'd been trying to force them in against their hinges. His face burned red with angry realization.

Swallowing his embarrassment, Webb slowly opened the doors in the conventional fashion. Now back inside, he really wanted to go back to his room and stew for a while, but he knew that would only cause his anger to fester and grow. He could always go and talk with Uncle Mike or Mathias, but he was afraid they would be too busy or accuse him of whining. Well, Mathias would probably be subtler than that, but Uncle Mike was always direct. What Webb needed was someone more objective, someone who could understand his point of view.

"Come in, Webb," boomed the Gaelic voice, freezing Webb's fist before it could knock upon the door.

Webb stepped in self-consciously, his mind racing over what he was going to say now that he was there. He turned to find the Willkeeper diligently writing in one of his many books, the green lamp still the only source of light in the vast room.

The Willkeeper looked up, his beard and hair just as disheveled as it was the first time Webb had met him. "Just finishing up another day in the life," he said, winking at Webb in the process.

"How do you do it?" asked Webb.

"Do what, Webb?"

"Write and write and write. I mean you record everyone's life day after day. It gives me hand cramps just thinking about it," he said, unconsciously rubbing his right hand in the process.

The Willkeeper smiled and gently shut the volume before him. "Is that what you really came to talk to me about?" he asked as the book sailed away from the table to an anonymous bookshelf in the back of the room.

Webb shrugged uncomfortably.

The Willkeeper smiled. "Well, if you must know. I enjoy what I do. It's all I've ever known and all I ever want to do. It is my passion, not my burden."

Webb nodded and began to fidget around the room.

"Kane a little hard on you this morning?"

"Already recorded, huh?" replied Webb, defeated.

"Of course."

"The guy's a scarfaced jerk," Webb muttered.

The Willkeeper pursed his lips. "Kane is not all what you believe. Yes, he can be obstinate, elitist, and overtly opinionated, but he is also a member of the Glorian Council, and that should tell you something."

"Tells me he pulled a number on the selection committee," Webb responded sarcastically.

"Hardly, boyo. Hardly. Kane has sacrificed more for Glorian than you will ever know."

The words were simple, but it was the tone that silenced Webb's rebuttal. He instead turned away from the Willkeeper's stare and feigned interest in the books in the higher reaches of the room.

"You're new here, Webb, and greatly confused. You've got varying realities vying to tell you what is real and what isn't. You need to understand that everything done within Glorian's realm is for a greater reason and nothing is done for spite or any other such petty cause. In time, you will come to understand the validity of it."

"Yeah, so I've been told," Webb sighed. "But if everything is so high and mighty around here, then why does scarface treat me like dirt?"

"First, it does you no good at all to refer to Kane as *scarface*. That is only going to exacerbate your anger. Second, have you not realized the whole reason for his baiting you?"

Webb went silent, his mind racing over the entire session that morning, but nothing stuck out save for Kane's infuriating jibes. "Maybe I'm a slow learner."

"Maybe you just don't just want to hear it?" chided the Willkeeper. "Don't you remember Kane's comment about the prominence of anger in your gift?"

"He should talk! *He's* not exactly Mr. Happy! Besides, he was acting like a jerk the whole time and got what he deserved."

"There it is," replied the Willkeeper, standing up and moving from around his desk. "The famous Webb Thompson temper. Got you in trouble more than once in the living world, didn't it? And now it has trailed you here! Just another unappealing echo that has found its way into the Dark Lands. We're getting more and more such echoes, you know? I believe it is another sign of the Dark Man's increasing power, but that's neither here nor there."

He put his arm around Webb as the boy grimaced silently in the shame of being lectured, especially by someone who knew his entire life history.

"This might sound cliché, but there are certain emotional echoes that are caustic to Glorian. Anger is one of the more prominent ones and Kane was trying to furrow out exactly how entrenched anger is within your gift. If your gift can only be effectively tapped with anger, then it is not much use. In fact, it becomes a threat to us."

"As long as I use it against the Vindicadives what does it matter?"

The Willkeeper let loose with a *hrmph*. "Has anger *ever* led you to a good place, Webb?"

"Depends," Webb said hastily. Giving the question a moment longer to percolate, Webb followed up with an apathetic shake of his head.

"It's just a dark spiral, one that makes you too vulnerable to the Dark Man. Kane has never been subtle in his methodologies, but they are effective. He found in you what Mathias, what the entire Council in fact, suspected."

The entire Council? Webb suddenly felt very naked. Was he *that* transparent?

"You've got to control your anger and turn it into something else, some feeling more productive. That's the only way your gift can be fully utilized. That is what Kane was trying to tell you in his own unique way. But it's up to you to do it."

"I still don't think I understand."

"You will in time, boyo. I have faith in you," smiled the Willkeeper. "Now, if you don't mind, I've got a few more histories to record," he said, motioning over to his desk. "Besides, I think you've gotten off your chest what you needed. Go eat some lunch and relax."

Webb nodded and started to walk out of the room.

"And Webb?" called the Willkeeper.

"Yes?"

"Thanks for stopping by. It does get lonely here after some time."

Webb offered the Willkeeper a smile in return and then walked out into the hallway, his mood slightly elevated.

His stomach was in full rumble mode when he smelled the cafeteria and he was almost unbearably hungry by the time he'd crossed its threshold. His mind's eye was locked on images of spiced meatloaf and tender steamed vegetables.

Webb walked to the center of the room and began to look for his sister and Raven, but in the process caught a glimpse of the blond-headed boy he'd seen the previous evening. He looked up at Webb and smiled. Webb nodded and proceeded over to him, a plate of meatloaf and vegetables concurrently appearing across from the young man, prepared exactly as Webb had anticipated.

"Hi. I'm Webb," he said offering his hand.

The young man shook it enthusiastically. "I'm Caleb."

Webb sat down, noticing that Caleb was enjoying a hamburger and french fries. "They've got great burgers here," Webb offered.

"Everything here is great. How can it *not* be, if you really think about it?" Caleb responded while shoving a few fries in his mouth.

Webb shrugged. He guessed he was right.

"You and your sister had quite the scare last night, didn't you?"

"You could say that."

"Is it true that was your *second* run-in with the Whoop-Dingers in two days?"

"Yeah, we aren't the luckiest people at Glorian," answered Webb.

"I don't know. Might even be kind of interesting," responded Caleb evenly.

"Not *interesting*. Eerie. Scary. Horrifying. Those are the words I'd use. Trust me on that."

Caleb gave the impression that he was considering Webb's statement before quietly going back to his hamburger.

"So, how long have you been here?" Webb asked.

"I don't know. It all seems to flow together over time, one day melding right into another. I stopped keeping track of the time long ago. I died when I was eighteen, sometime in 1973, if that gives you any idea."

"So, you've been here a while," replied Webb, trying to avoid Caleb's nonchalant use of the word, *died*. "Well, you don't look a day over twenty," he added jokingly.

"Time flies," mused Caleb. "French fry?" he offered.

Webb shook his head. "No thanks, I had fries the other day," he declined politely.

"Suit yourself. That meatloaf does look good though," Caleb continued to banter. "I believe I had meatloaf just last week."

Caleb seemed nice, but he almost seemed too content in a way that unnerved Webb. After poking at the carrots with his fork, he decided to try to broach the subject. "Hey, Caleb?"

"Yeah?"

"You can tell me to shut up at any time, but you seem kind of happy about being here," said Webb, not able to contain his curiosity. "Why is that?"

"No, I don't mind talking about it," Caleb smiled. "You're right. I do like being here."

"You *like* it here?" Webb repeated.

"Yeah. Want another shocker?"

"Sure, why not?"

"I like it here much better than I did the living world."

Webb had just taken a swig of soda when Caleb's answer caused him to cough it back up through his nose.

"I don't think I've ever gotten *that* kind of a reaction," Caleb laughed.

Webb wiped off his face and looked back up at Caleb. "Glad I could amuse you," he replied embarrassingly. "Now, that we've broken the ice, would you mind telling me why you like it here so much? Why you'd rather be here than back home?"

Caleb took a bite of his hamburger and appeared to ponder the appropriate response. "I guess it's just a matter of perspective. Quality of life here versus back there."

"Quality of life? What do you mean? This place is basically a giant prison that gets attacked by monsters trying to kill you every single day!" Webb protested.

Caleb made a cynical smirk. "Tell me, Webb, were you into athletics back there, in the living world? You know, sports and the like? Football? Basketball?"

"Yeah, I played football on the team. I was a safety, defensive specialist," Webb proudly replied.

"Fun, huh? What about girlfriends?" continued Caleb.

"Yeah. The usual. I mean, just a couple; they didn't end up working out though. Kind of embarrassing, really. Why do you ask?"

"You see, I never had any of that," replied Caleb. "Never could've."

"What do you mean?" asked Webb.

"I was born with a condition that confined me to a wheelchair, amongst other problems. Don't bother asking me what it was; I don't care to recall it. Regardless, for nearly twenty years, I was what I was. I never knew the joy of running down a hillside. Never knew the intimacy of a slow walk with a girl. The only thing I ever knew was the cold steel of my chair, the awkward stares and people glancing away as I met their gaze... And that got old real quick."

Despite the bitterness behind the words, Webb heard no animosity in Caleb's voice. It was all recounted very matter-of-factly, but it didn't make Webb feel any less ashamed for his brazenness. "I'm sorry."

Caleb suddenly looked bemused. "Most rush to finish their meals and then leave in some type of self-imposed shame after I tell them my tale. You're the first to actually appear to slow down eating."

"Oh, is that good or bad?" Webb asked.

"I don't have many friends here. Back home, I didn't have many friends either. Most people felt uncomfortable around me. And I could never figure out if others were only being nice to me just because I was disabled. I just figured that same vibe had crossed over to here in its own ugly little echo. I was so used to eating and doing everything else on my own. It feels… good to have someone to talk with, I mean someone who isn't obliged to talk with you as a counselor. And even then, being alone is still more preferable than trying to talk with someone like Kane."

"You have to deal with scarface too!?" erupted Webb, as if he had heard nothing except for Caleb's last sentence.

Caleb laughed out loud at the moniker. "Yes, of course. He is the key facilitator for all Dispersers."

"And you're a Disperser?"

"Yes! You too?"

"That's what I'm told," replied Webb, taking a large bite of his meatloaf in the process.

"I haven't seen you during lessons."

"I've only had one lesson and it was a one-on-one with Kane."

"Yeah, the first few times are private, then you move on to the group settings with the rest who share your gift," spoke Caleb, beaming now that they'd found a similarity to bond over. "It's just the way they acclimate you here. Don't want too much too soon, or it'll go over your head."

"So, are the group settings like school or something?" Webb asked as he pictured a high school classroom being kept at rigid attention by Kane.

"No," answered Caleb. "Not really. It's held in a classroom-type place, but it's not like ol' *scarface*," Caleb let loose a laugh, "or any of the other facilitators are up at the chalkboard lecturing or anything like that. It's more like a place to practice, share, and refine abilities. You'll see."

Webb shrugged. "When do I join you all?"

"Soon, I would expect."

"So, is Kane his typical bitter self in the group-settings too?"

"Pretty much, but that's just him. Some who have been here longer than I have tell me that he wasn't always like that," replied Caleb, eagerly taking another bite of his burger. A slice of pickle fell from the sandwich with a soft splat on his plate.

"Really? Kane used to be a *pleasant* person? I find that hard to believe," said Webb, eyeing the pickle. "The guy is a… premium sour jerk."

"A lot of people call him a lot of things, but from what I understand, something happened in the War of the Sentinels that changed him. That's when he got his scar and became what he is today," said Caleb, his eyes looking off to the side as he tried to recall exactly what he'd heard.

"*The War of Sentinels?*"

"Not up on your Dark Land's history?" asked Caleb teasingly. "There used to be a gifted sect in the Dark Lands known as Sentinels. Before they were all killed in the war, that is."

Webb shook his head. "Wait, what's a *Sentinel?*"

"They were great warriors who possessed every imaginable gift in the Dark Lands, much more than just being able to disperse like you or I. That's why they were the true protectors of Glorian—the first line of defense before anyone else."

"So this War of the Sentinels, was it one of the thousand-year wars?" asked Webb, recalling what Mathias had told him.

"No," answered Caleb. "That's the thing. The Dark Man launched an unprecedented offensive against Glorian, not in synch with the normal thousand year time frames. It was an ambush, in order to surprise and eradicate the Sentinels. And he basically did. It was one of the greatest battles ever fought in the Dark Lands. The bloodiest with the greatest losses ever recorded, from what I understand. So, it wasn't a thousand-year war per se, but it might as well have been."

"That bad?"

"Don't know the full details, but yeah, that bad," responded Caleb bleakly. "I mean, the Sentinels were basically wiped out. And they were the best of the best."

"And that's when Kane became the charming person we all know and love?"

"That's the rumor. After the Sentinels had fallen, he was one of the last ones left facing off against the Dark Man. I hear it was the Dark Man who 'blinked,' if you get my drift. There was a standoff and eventually the Dark Man chose to retreat with the remainder of his forces."

"I don't find that hard to believe at all. Even the Dark Man knows not to mess with Kane," Webb laughed, but he begrudgingly felt a feeling of newfound respect for the man, albeit slight.

Caleb nodded. "Anyway, he's the lead facilitator for dispersing. I'd try and get along with him."

Webb sighed as depressing images of Kane breathing down his neck for all eternity flooded his thoughts. Who knew, maybe it would only be the next hundred years or so. His gaze shifted towards a pair sitting down across the room and his eyes focused upon something almost just as frustrating. There was Sundown, eating and chatting merrily with Badego, the grinning snake oil salesman. He groaned aloud.

CHAPTER FIFTEEN

A PECULIAR ALLIANCE

"It's like I'm my own personalized rewind button!" Sundown exclaimed in between globby bites of mint chocolate chip ice cream. She was too ecstatic for such standard lunch fare as pizza, burgers, or chicken. Instead, she had opted to take a page out of Iggy's book and have something a little more decadent.

"It is a grand gift, and one you should relish," Badego replied, humoring her youthful excitement.

Sundown was suddenly overcome by a childish urge to hear Badego praise her gift one more time. Without thinking, she began to draw time back, stopping it right before Badego had complimented her.

"It is a grand gift, and one you should relish," she heard Badego say again.

Sundown snickered and smiled mischievously.

"What?" asked Badego, catching her sudden grin.

"Nothing," replied Sundown, regaining her composure. It was just so incredible to be able to do what she could—to reclaim time, with no one being the wiser.

Raven's dour mood while discussing the gift had made Sundown very self-conscious about expressing even the slightest measure of her excitement. Just to appease her, Sundown had said that she could understand how the gift could become burdensome, but she really felt that Raven was just being a bit melodramatic. How could changing what went wrong be a bad thing? Even if she messed up, she could do it over and over again, until she got everything right! It was what everyone always *wished* they could do. Maybe Raven was just perpetually a "Gloomy Gretchen," a personality unable to afford enjoyment in anything. During their sessions together, Sundown could rarely ever recall Raven cracking a smile.

"What's on your mind, Sundown?" asked Badego. "You suddenly look distant."

"Oh, I don't know…" she replied. Then she added, "What is your gift, Badego?"

Badego paused and set down the apple he suddenly had in his hands. "I am an *Influencer*, but what does that have to do with my question?"

"What's an Influencer?" Sundown again ignored Badego's inquiry.

Badego shrugged. "Would you like me to show you?"

Sundown widened her eyes in anticipation and nodded.

Badego pursed his lips in contemplation and then grinned broadly at her. "*Laugh for me*," he hissed out.

Sundown was inexplicably overcome with the irresistible urge to laugh, and she did just that. She laughed quickly. She laughed slowly. She laughed every which way she had ever laughed in her life. She ran the entire vocal gambit, clutching her sides, her stomach beginning to hurt with each convulsion. Badego just sat there watching her, covering his mouth with his napkin in stifled amusement.

"*Stop laughing*," Badego finally hissed out, his own genuine laughter at the girl's influence now becoming almost uncontrollable.

Sundown immediately stopped in mid-guffaw. She flushed red and looked over the cafeteria, embarrassed at who might have witnessed her display. When no one seemed to notice the scene, she turned her attention back towards Badego in great irritation. ·

"You could have simply *told* me," she said thinly.

"No one saw," assured Badego, "And even if they had, I could have told them to forget that they saw you. An Influencer has some rather grand abilities as well."

Sundown begrudgingly accepted what she perceived as his own weak attempt at an apology. "...So you can make people do things they don't want to do?"

Badego nodded. "Most. A few people are strong enough to withstand my 'suggestions,' but I can give them a royal headache for their troubles," he joked.

"And you can make them forget things as well?" Sundown probed.

"Yes," he replied, finally taking a bite of his apple. "Usually."

"Interesting," was Sundown's sole reply.

"Now, why all these questions? What's all this about?" he asked.

"Are you proud of your gift?" she responded, answering his question with a question once again.

"Yes," answered Badego in near frustration, sighing aloud.

Sundown smiled nervously. "Well, it just seems that Raven isn't too pleased with being a Reclaimer. She almost treats it like a curse and she wants me to treat it the same way too."

"Ah, so *that's* what this is about? Validation. You want validation for your feelings?"

"I guess so," mumbled Sundown. "I just don't understand why Raven has to be such a spoilsport."

"Well, Raven has a more... subdued personality. She isn't overly excitable. Doesn't mean she is a 'spoilsport,' as you so put it. We have all kinds here and that's what makes the dynamics so harmonious. Despite our various backgrounds and gifts, we can all cooperate together to perform our roles."

Sundown subtly rolled her eyes, anticipating an upcoming lecture about appreciating differences. Rather, she was pleasantly surprised by what Badego said next.

"That doesn't mean your gift isn't special though, and you should be very proud of it. There aren't many Reclaimers here, you know; it takes a certain kind of great soul to be a Reclaimer."

Sundown perked up.

"As I said, your gift is a grand one and you should not be ashamed to use it. There are many doors, so to speak, that your gift can open that will make you privy to wonders others will never know. Don't be selfish with it, but don't be too selfless either."

"What are you saying?" Sundown replied, a puzzled look crossing her face.

"Let's just say that sometimes what you perceive as an obligation to Glorian can blind you to the obligation you have to be true to yourself. Don't be misguided by misplaced loyalty." Badego punctuated his cryptic response with another crunch of his apple.

"Okay," Sundown replied hesitantly. She really didn't get anything he had just said besides the part about being proud of her gift, but she didn't care. All she'd wanted to hear was that she could be happy about her gift; that part made her feel better.

"Now, this little conversation was just between us. Don't go telling Raven this, as she might get cross with me. We aren't supposed to intrude on one another's charges, but given that you needed a little reassurance, I saw no harm in it this time. We have a deal?" Badego asked.

"Sure," Sundown replied.

What was there to tell Raven anyway? Badego had just been talking a bunch of nonsense.

CHAPTER SIXTEEN

A LITTLE TALK

Webb watched Badego depart the cafeteria from across the room through seething eyes. Was he the only one who distrusted the man? His sister certainly seemed to think him quite the charmer given the way she had been acting during lunch, laughing like a madwoman the way she was. Well, *he* wasn't amused and he was going let Badego know how he felt.

"Excuse me," he said absently to Caleb as he stood from their table. He brushed by a few residents on their way to their seats and followed Badego out into the hallway.

"Badego!" he thundered out.

The older man turned, a meek little expression on his face. "Yes, Webb?"

"Good memory," he replied in annoyance. "We need to have a little talk."

Badego looked tickled at Webb's irritation. "Sure. Go ahead."

"I don't appreciate your pretending to be my sister's best friend. I know what you're up to," Webb accused.

Badego paused, furrowing his brow in perplexity. "And what exactly *am* I up to?"

The question, though so very simple and obvious, caught Webb completely off guard. What exactly did he suspect Badego of? Aside from his screaming instincts, there was actually nothing overt that warranted Webb's extreme dislike or suspicion of the man. Badego had not done or said anything even remotely unpleasant to him or anyone else. To the contrary, he had managed to pull some sincere laughter from his sister during lunch and that was something Webb hadn't seen in a while. Why then, did he perceive the man so negatively? Was he just being an overbearing, overprotective big brother? Without the words to back himself up, his jaw went slack.

"Webb, I again ask why you feel I am so threatening?"

"I-I just know," Webb stammered out, unable to answer.

"Ooookay," drawled Badego sarcastically.

Webb's eyes began to blink rapidly from the frustration. It made him even angrier that his idiosyncratic little tic couldn't be controlled even in the afterlife.

"Webb, you're new to the Dark Lands. There is quite a bit of the living world you still have to shed to understand the here and now."

"I've been told that one already," Webb interrupted.

"Being protective of one's sister," Badego continued empathetically, "is a very admirable trait, but there is no need to be so protective of her here in Glorian. We all are on the same side. There are no hidden agendas. It might go against your nature, but you are just going to have to *trust me*."

"Sorry. I guess it's just not in my nature, like you said," Webb answered defiantly.

"I see," Badego replied, momentarily disarmed by the cold response. "Well then, perhaps we can agree to a truce that might lead to a better understanding of one another?"

"I'll think about it."

"Very well," Badego nodded. The older man then turned slowly on his heels, casting one more puzzled look upon Webb before moving away.

Webb's eyes continued to blink hard, but this time, it was due to the sharp headache that had suddenly come upon him. He began to rub his temples.

"That's what you get for being so angry all the time," called a voice from behind him.

Webb turned to find Sundown staring at him, her hands resting on her hips in a matronly fashion. His eyes squinted as the headache continued to pound inside his skull like a bass drum. "...What are you talking about?" he groaned.

"Your headache. You always rub your temples like that when you get a headache."

"Well, I sure didn't get it from being angry," he replied in annoyance.

"Sure you did," replied Sundown smugly. "You get so mad and lose it and all that angry blood has nowhere else to go but your head."

"I'm *not* angry," Webb replied with a slight grimace.

"Could've fooled me the way you took after Badego."

Webb ceased rubbing his temples and leveled a stare at his sister. He hadn't thought she'd witnessed the exchange. "Sorry, Sunny, I just don't trust the guy."

"What do you mean you don't trust him? What's there to not trust?" she pressed.

"I... I don't know. He's just... I just don't trust him, Sunny!"

Her eyes narrowed in frustration. "Ugh, that's not even an answer! I don't see what's wrong with you. Are you just jealous that I'm making friends? That I'm getting along? I don't get you sometimes, Webb!" she cried. "He's so nice and he's really helped me feel at home here!"

Webb didn't know if it was the headache furiously eating away at his skull or the casualness of his sister's statement, but the comment infuriated him.

"Feel at *home* here!?" Webb shrieked. His head felt like it had just rolled over a speed bump. "Home!? I am so sick and tired of everyone glossing over what is really happening here! Sundown, we are *dead*. Both of us are dead. Everyone here is dead! We are *far* from home!"

The tempo of his headache began to rage harder as his heart raced, causing his eyes to squeeze shut. In the blackness, his anger flared even greater, spurring the continuation of the tirade pouring from his lips.

"Are you actually stupid, or are you just playing dumb like everyone else? We're caught in some weird, alternate world where almost everyone and everything outside of this castle wants to murder us, but no one besides me really seems to appreciate that!"

He let loose an audible groan as his knees buckled from the pain, eyes still closed. He could no longer tell if Sundown was still there as she had gone conspicuously quiet, but he continued with his verbal volleys none the less.

"So, you can continue to 'feel at home' with jerks like your beloved Badego and pretend we're at some kind of summer camp, and that those Whoop-Dingers that almost ate us are just hungry little raccoons or something. As for me, I am *not* going to sit around saying everything is fine."

By the time the words had finished spewing from his mouth, Webb wished he could suck them all back in again, but it was far too late for that. He wearily opened his eyes and the shocked look on his sister's face told him as much.

"*You're* the jerk, Webb!" she exclaimed before running off down the hallway.

Webb tried to call after her, but she disappeared before he could work his aching brain around the beginnings of an apology. All he could do was sit down against the wall with his head in his hands as the tears flowed through his fingers.

He didn't know how long he was cradled there, pain and regret hammering him into nauseous despair. He heard the crossing tracks and mumbling voices of people in a blur as they moved in and out of the cafeteria. A few people stopped before him, unsure if they should say something before moving on to let him be. He thought he heard Caleb ask if he was okay, but it had seemed so distant that it might have been just a dream. It was sometime during this haze that he felt a hand rest on his shoulder, drawing him out of his self-pity. His aching eyes looked up to find Mathias gazing benignly upon him.

"I understand that you've had a bad day."

"You could say that," grimaced Webb as Mathias helped him stand up. "And this headache isn't making it any better."

"Well, I might be able to do something about your headache at the very least," replied Mathias. "Take a deep breath."

Webb followed the old man's instruction, willing to do anything to rid himself of the unbearable pounding.

"Now, concentrate on your pain and then slowly exhale."

He was initially dubious, but the result was mystifying. As Webb exhaled, he could literally feel the throbbing in his head begin to seep out of him, like water spilling from a bottle tipped on its side. When the last rush of air had left his mouth, the pain was completely extinguished.

"That was awesome," Webb blurted out.

"A headache is merely an imbalance. To remedy it, all that needs to be done is to allow that imbalance to flow out of you. It's like removing the top of a teakettle and letting all of the steam flow out unencumbered. In your case, it seems your emotions were unsettled, at odds with one another."

Webb cast his eyes down glumly. "Yeah, I guess so. Thank you for your help, Mathias."

The old man smiled gently. "Now that all is well again, let's talk about your session with Kane this morning," he said, putting his arm around Webb's shoulders and leading him away from the cafeteria. "Want to tell me about it?"

"I'm sure Kane's already told you," Webb answered sullenly.

"Kane did indeed come and see me this morning after your first session."

"Probably said I was unruly, unworthy, undisciplined and let's not forget, *impetuous*."

Mathias stifled a laugh. "Yes, he might have called you that once or twice, as he does all of the younger Glorians. Of course, you and your sister are the youngest here."

"The *youngest*? Oh, that's great," Webb almost laughed. "The youngest and therefore the *most* impetuous!"

"Don't worry. You're not too much younger, just slightly."

"Yeah, I'm sure Kane appreciates that difference," Webb said disdainfully.

"For his own reasons, Kane is very harsh on our younger Glorians."

"Let me guess, anyone a hundred years old or less?" Webb scoffed.

"Not *that* bad," Mathias smiled. "I know that you've had conversations with the Willkeeper and your new friend, Caleb. They've both tried to council you on why Kane is the way he is. Obviously, they failed since I can still feel much hostility in you towards him."

"Can you blame me?"

"Blame is not the issue. Understanding is."

Webb felt his already bad mood descend even deeper. Even Mathias was against him. He started to beg off from the conversation when he noted they were in front of Mathias' room. He waved Webb inside the oval chamber before he could protest.

There were two bowls of ice cream on the table. One Webb readily recognized as his favorite: chocolate chip. The other was a smooth, light brown concoction sprinkled with what appeared to be chunks of caramel and chocolate.

"Java chip," explained Mathias. "My favorite."

Webb sat down in front of the chocolate chip ice cream and though he had no appetite, he gingerly took a spoonful out of courtesy for the meal. The moment its creamy texture touched his tongue and slid down his throat, however, a small feeling of happiness bubbled up from within him.

"It is impossible to not feel good when you eat ice cream. Impossible, I tell you," Mathias said as he sat down and took a large spoon himself.

Webb nodded in agreement, again feeling the security of the room envelop him. He felt much more at ease already. He took another bite of the ice cream; he had forgotten how much he really enjoyed chocolate chip.

"Now, back to the discussion at hand. Kane does indeed have some concerns, but he also says that he sees some promise in you."

"Some?"

"That's quite the compliment coming from Kane. You need understand that Kane's attitude and actions are steeped solely in his concern for Glorian and not in some trivial dislike or vendetta. He isn't as a cold a man as you think." Mathias steadied his eyes on Webb.

"I've been told that too many times today," he replied exasperatedly.

Mathias nodded empathetically. "If I were in your position, I'd think the same way. Alas, it has been thousands of years since I was in your position. Let me just suggest this to you," the old man paused, measuring his words carefully. "We are all shaped by what has transpired in our respective pasts. Sometimes events can cause us such unspeakable pain that in order to survive, we just simply remove ourselves from anything that would allow that same pain to ever again surface."

"I guess," Webb muttered.

"Let me give you a more personal example," Mathias offered, to counter the boy's disingenuous tone. "Your dog, Daisy. When she died, you felt incredible pain, didn't you?"

"Yes," responded Webb.

"So much pain that you vowed that you'd never own another dog again?"

Webb nodded gently.

"Then, it was more acceptable to you to never know the love of another dog than to experience the pain of losing one again," Mathias said.

"So, what did Kane lose?" Webb asked, hedging in his question.

"Ah, that is for Kane himself to disclose to you. So," Mathias paused, "I trust that when Kane comes calling tomorrow, you will do your best to resist your prejudices and try to learn?"

"Why can't *you* teach me? Aren't you my counselor?"

"For your gift, there is no one better than Kane to facilitate your training, especially given your disposition to anger," replied Mathias taking another bite of his java chip dessert.

"Can we talk about my supposed 'disposition to anger' that everyone keeps mentioning?"

"Again, we are in Kane's territory, but I will share this with you. It is partially that your age predisposes you to terrible anger. Not enough to make you a pariah to Glorian, but it does need to be controlled. Kane will help you with that."

"By making me angrier?"

"Just trust me, Webb. His methods work," said Mathias, ending the discussion. "Now, we do have one more matter to attend to. Your apparent distrust of Badego."

Webb's mouth went slack. What did Mathias *not* know?

"At the risk of sounding tired, I must reinforce that you are in the Dark Lands now, not the living world. You're going to have to develop a trust for *everyone* within Glorian."

"My instincts tell me to do otherwise," replied Webb without thinking. He was somewhat surprised that he'd challenged Mathias, even if it was something as superficial as this. He trusted the old gentleman; he just didn't think he was right in this case.

"Instincts can be a good thing when honed properly. But sometimes, they can be misguided."

Webb said nothing in response.

"I know it is difficult, Webb. Orienting one's self to the Dark Lands while simultaneously shedding the echoes of the living world can be a strenuous task, but it will happen. You just have to let it."

Webb nodded in feigned agreement while looking down at his now empty bowl; his reflection watched him solemnly from the cream-covered porcelain. Despite what everyone kept telling him, he just had the feeling that some echoes didn't need to be shed.

CHAPTER SEVENTEEN

BETRAYAL

Webb had gloomily gone looking for Sundown after leaving Mathias' office. His reluctance stemmed partly from the exhaustion that was starting to plague him, but mostly from the idea of having to apologize to his little sister. He knew he was wrong for exploding the way he did, but at the time, he had felt justified. Now he felt nothing but embarrassment—an emotion which he was unfortunately starting to become very familiar with these days.

Apologies weren't his strong suit. He'd rather just forget about past transgressions and move on, but his sister didn't see things that way; to her, apologies were a requisite to moving on. So he had gone up and down the hallways looking for Sundown. When he couldn't find her walking around in the open, he finally surrendered to the fact that he might just have to go to her room and knock on the door. A trust of his instincts and a few turns later and he did that very thing, but to no avail. All that came from Sundown's room was silence.

He made another cursory search up and down the darkened hallway, but he neither saw nor heard anything. It was approaching dinnertime by now, so he imagined that she, as well as almost everyone else, had settled in the cafeteria. He definitely wasn't going to go in and apologize to Sundown there—not in front of Raven, and most certainly not in front of Badego. He didn't have the constitution for that. No, he decided he would skip dinner once again in favor of his room. Apologies could wait until tomorrow.

The sweet rush of familiarity greeted him as he opened the door. He looked to his bed to find that Gustafson had apparently left while he was out. He frowned at the absence, feeling even lonelier suddenly. The cat was kind of growing on him. As if on cue, a "meow" broke the silence.

Webb looked curiously around the bedroom. No Gustafson, but the sound had definitely come from somewhere in his room. He looked in the closet and then under his bed, but there was nothing there either. As if to tease him, another "meow" called out. He paused thoughtfully and then slowly looked up. There, posing regally on the ceiling, sat Gustafson looking up—or down as it were—at Webb.

"I'm not going to ask how you did that," Webb replied as he fell backwards onto his bed. He flinched as he landed on something hard on his side and realized that he'd just lain on his jacket pocket full of Kane's stupid marbles. Sighing in frustration at the sore reminder, he grabbed the fistful of marbles and placed them in a pencil cup on his nightstand before flopping back down onto the bed.

Gustafson watched him from the ceiling all the while. He let loose a stream of what sounded like chirps before standing on all fours and walking down the nearest wall to pounce onto the bed with him. He then settled the front of his body on Webb's chest, expecting to receive a petting. Webb let loose a slight groan at Gustafson's weight, but he nevertheless began to stroke the cat's silky black fur, appreciating the company.

"You're just full of surprises," Webb said while scratching behind the Felix's ears. "So tell me. Mathias says there are quite a few of your type running around here. So, why are you the only one I've seen? Are the rest of your brothers and sisters sleeping on ceilings too?" Webb chuckled.

He actually found it very therapeutic to pet Gustafson, every stroke of the animal's fur making him feel a little better. Gustafson, for his part, simply purred and stared attentively back at him with an intelligent glint in his green eyes. It almost seemed to Webb that the creature was going to speak at any moment, not that it would have really surprised Webb if he had, but nothing of the sort happened. He finished rubbing the feline's neck and ears and then closed his eyes, letting himself sink into the comfort of his pillow.

Webb suddenly started in bed, unsettling Gustafson and causing the cat to raise its hackles. It took a few moments to register what had spooked him out of his half-sleep. He checked his clock. It was the sudden hum of Glorian closing down and locking for the impending six o'clock onslaught.

The attack started a minute later. Webb looked over at Gustafson who had settled himself at the far end of the bed. The cat's eyes were darting alertly with concentration, his ears perked as the screams and tormented sounds howled around them. Webb laid his head back on his pillow once more, pulling it around his ears in an attempt to take the edge off the aural onslaught. He had only endured these assaults for a few days and it was already beginning to tax his psyche. How had those who'd been at Glorian for so many years managed to keep their sanity?

A new sound suddenly joined the dissonance, a vibration that might otherwise have been concealed by the incessant pounding and shrieking, had Webb not been lying in bed, pressed tightly against his bedroom wall. He lifted his head up off of his pillow, the vibration now turning into a low hum. His face went ghostly pale. He knew that sound. Glorian was being unlocked.

Webb leapt off of the bed and ran to his door. Throwing it open, he rushed out into the hallway, Gustafson dashing ahead of him into the shadows. If memory served, one of the keys that locked down the fort was just down the passageway from his room. He sprinted in that direction while various bedroom doorways timidly opened behind him, their occupants stepping out awash in a clear mixture of curiosity and fear.

As Webb drew towards the keyhole, he saw a shadow splayed upon the stony wall hurriedly running away. Was that who had unlocked Glorian? But why would anyone do such a thing? Webb quickly looked around the keyhole for the key itself, but there was nothing. Then on the floor, he caught a slight sheen in the darkness, light glinting off something metallic and black. It was the key.

Actually, it was only part of the key. It had been broken cleanly in half. He peered inside the keyhole and found the rest of it, snapped flush with the wall. Webb clawed at the keyhole fruitlessly for a few seconds and gritted his teeth, but kept his composure, aware that several Glorians were starting to mass around him. The hum was still reverberating; Glorian was opening itself further.

He spun around, looking at the curious faces encircling him. "The key has been broken off in the lock!" Webb shouted to the crowd. "Where is the next keyhole?"

"Right next to the entrance! Way down there," pointed a middle-aged man who'd just come from his room.

"Of course," Webb said ironically. He hurried down the hallway towards the entrance door, his footsteps made fleet by his fear of the monsters outside and by his anticipation of catching the culprit who had done this. Most of the Glorians would still be at dinner right now, so the hallways would be relatively empty. He rounded the corner and almost ran directly into Caleb. So much for his theory.

"What are you doing here, Caleb?" he asked as he halted in mid-stride.

"I heard the noises," Caleb huffed out, his eyes frozen absently towards the doorway in confusion.

"I'd get out of here right now!" Webb shouted as he sped away. He made a quick glance back to find that Caleb was still standing there. He signaled for him to move, but Caleb either didn't see or didn't care to heed his warning.

Webb turned back to the approaching doorway. The closer he got, the more it seemed to be *breathing*, heaving in and out. But doors didn't breathe—something was pushing on it from outside, trying to force itself through.

He was only a few feet from the keyhole when a hand abruptly clutched him from behind. He whirled around, half-expecting to encounter a translucent horror.

"Uncle Mike!" Webb shouted, relieved to see the man. "Someone's opening the doors!"

"I know, Webb!" he exclaimed, brushing past his nephew. He grabbed a key from the wall and inserted it into the keyhole, making a swift turn. The hum was momentarily interrupted by a convergence of clicking noises, but then the rumble reengaged as the fortress locked back down.

"What happened?" Webb asked breathlessly.

"I don't know," his uncle panted. "Mathias and the rest of the Council should be here shortly. They might have some answers."

Webb looked down the hallway at the Glorians gathering around, the noise of their frantic conversations adding to the already confused atmosphere. Standing behind them all was Caleb, unmoving and solitary, his face still strangely unreadable.

"Who could have done this?" Webb asked, his eyes locked on Caleb.

Uncle Mike shook his head in disbelief. "It's never happened before—at least not as far as I've known," he replied.

Suddenly a jarring creak announced itself over the surrounding din. Webb and his uncle turned simultaneously towards the large entryway doors.

"What *was* that?" Webb asked.

Uncle Mike reached his hand out and slowly pushed Webb back, placing himself between the doorway and his nephew. "Get back to your room, Webb, and stay there until I come and get you."

"Uncle Mike-"

"Get back now." His tone was uncompromising.

Webb took a few steps back, his eyes still locked on the doorframe as it started to again give the illusion of breathing. A twinge of horror coldly wrapped itself around his stomach. Something had managed to creep inside Glorian's defenses before they managed to lock it down; they'd gotten between the closed walls and the buckling doorway before them.

He took another step back as the doors started to groan, the lumber moaning and splintering in protest. Webb looked to his uncle, standing defiantly before the great doors, his body's weight resting tensely on his cane as splinters popped and showered around him. Despite the terror, Webb felt an unfettered sense of pride as he watched his uncle standing so fearlessly before the looming assault.

The doors continued to buckle and groan, each pop making Webb take another step back. Then, the breaking point was reached.

The doors exploded as countless Whoop-Dingers spewed into Glorian, screaming their animal cries. Webb watched as his uncle dropped his cane and shoved both arms forward, creating a shockwave that slammed several of the monsters to the ground. Several more, however, were able to slip by their fallen comrades unscathed.

"Webb, GO!" his uncle screamed.

"What about Sundown!?"

"She's on the other side of Glorian. Someone will be there for her. Now get away from here!"

Webb turned and ran. Where he'd go now, he had no idea. What protection would the flimsy door to his room provide against Whoop-Dingers that had been able to shred the enormous entrance doors? The creatures were raging all around him. Some Glorians were standing their ground, attempting to fight off the creatures; others were fleeing to areas they no doubt had long planned for in case of emergencies like this. As he watched the people run or fight, Webb didn't know who was foolish and who was brave. Hadn't Mathias and Kane said that these creatures were frighteningly powerful?

Webb instinctively turned to find a Whoop-Dinger poised to swallow him. Webb ducked to the ground as the creature, hurtling from its own momentum, shot past him, leaving a slimy trail in its wake. Webb rolled over and got to his feet. He scurried onward as the echoes of battle roared behind him.

Ahead, he watched as a middle-aged man, the one who had only minutes before pointed Webb in the direction of the entryway, engaged a Whoop-Dinger. The man's actions were smooth and controlled.

He launched an incredible volley of repulsion waves at the creature, knocking it further and further back with each strike.

Webb found himself entranced by the telekinetic parry, momentarily forgetting about the terror that was all around him. Suddenly the creature let loose a shrill wail and made a feint towards him and then a lightning fast snaking move with its fluid body that the man was too slow to dodge. It caught him by the ankle and he was knocked to the ground hard and then it was all over. The Whoop-Dinger twisted and morphed and was upon him, consuming him whole. The man began to spastically mouth a scream and claw frantically within the soupy insides of the Whoop-Dinger. Then, his motions began to slow and his body drained and melted into a sick swirl of flesh, dissolving thereafter into of nothingness. The creature then began to fitfully convulse, vomiting forth another Whoop-Dinger from its watery shell. Where there had once been a singular monstrosity, there were now two.

Webb nauseously turned from the horror and made an erratic left turn down another corridor, attempting to distance himself from the Whoop-Dinger and its newest brood. His thoughts immediately rushed to Sundown. Had she secured herself in her room or, like so many others, had curiosity lured her out into the riot that was overwhelming the hallways? His mind racing distractedly, Webb lost his footing and spilled hard onto the stone floor.

Rising to his stinging knees, Webb heard growling coming up from behind him. He began to hurriedly crawl down the hallway looking for some sort of sanctuary to retreat within, but each door he came to was locked, nothing but silence greeting him through each one. Suddenly, the growl that had been pursuing him changed into a sickening squelching sound. Webb began to shiver and slowly turned around.

It was as if he was reliving a nightmare. A Whoop-Dinger was hovering before him, its fluid form metamorphosing into another banshee-like monstrosity, just like the beasts apparently always did before engulfing their prey. Webb impulsively stretched his hand out to repel the creature, but his mind could not focus. Nothing happened.

The Whoop-Dinger gave what appeared to be a malevolent wet chortle and moved forward.

Sundown hesitantly peered from her room into the darkness of the hallway. She held her breath, hoping to catch the slightest noise, but there was no sound for the moment. Minutes before, the macabre serenades of the six o'clock hour had been screeching away, but then they had inexplicably stopped cold. And it was not yet seven. She sensed there was something wrong, though she didn't know what it could be. Should she stay in her room or should she try to go out and ask someone what happened? Sundown had been torn over the question for several minutes, but she finally gathered her courage and stepped further out into the hallway.

This was the furthest from her room she had been since her confrontation with Webb that afternoon. She'd spent the whole time huddled away in her room, ignoring the many entreaties at her door, hashing and rehashing her brother's thorny words over and over again until she was numb.

It wasn't like what he'd said had been wrong. She more than realized their situation, more than appreciated their circumstances. It was just easier if she *didn't* fully acknowledge it, if she just sort of glossed over it all with kinder euphemisms and fun twists rather than taking on their reality directly. It had always worked for her back home, putting a flowery spin on the less than pleasant situations in life. A boyfriend didn't break up with her; *they just needed a break.* She didn't fail a test; *she just didn't do very well.* They weren't dead; they were just *in a situation.* But she wasn't at home anymore and the normal rules no longer applied. And now, she fully appreciated Webb's concerns—now that she knew something was terribly wrong within Glorian and that she was in real danger.

Every few seconds, she thought she heard a muffled scream echo from around the corner, but then it would be quickly swallowed up by the thick walls, making her wonder whether she had even heard anything at all or if it was all in her head. She swallowed again and began to cautiously walk in the direction of the sounds.

"I wouldn't go that way, child." The voice was soft, but made her jump none the less.

"Mathias?" she squinted. Sundown had only met him once before, with Raven, but his vocal cadence was unmistakable.

"Yes," he said, moving out of the shadows. "I would go back into your room and wait there. There is nothing you can do out here. The Council and a few others are rectifying the situation as we speak."

A shriek burst out of the darkness, jolting her once more.

"Go back to your room. This matter will be taken care of shortly," Mathias said reassuringly.

"Yes, Sundown," came a panting voice from behind her. "I'd do as Mathias suggested."

Sundown turned her head to find a very out-of-breath Badego approaching, his forehead gleaming with sweat.

"Where have you been, Badego?" asked Mathias.

"Other side of Glorian. I made my way over to see if the Whoop-Dingers had burst through here as well," he panted out.

Sundown's eyes grew alarmed. "Whoop-Dingers? In *here*?"

"Calm down. There has been only one breach. Several Whoop-Dingers managed to filter through, but they are all contained on the other side of Glorian," responded Mathias.

"And the one's remaining outside?" pressed Badego.

"Curious, I no longer heard their flailing once Glorian was again secured. I guess they all returned to the Dead Forest of Kenan-perhaps thinking they were not needed? I do not pretend to understand the machinations of those creatures," spoke Mathias calmly.

"Webb?" Sundown suddenly blurted out.

"I've no doubt he is being taken care of. Now, please return to your room, child." Mathias turned to Badego. "I need you to help me make sure the Whoop-Dingers are all eliminated from the grounds."

Badego followed along with Mathias while Sundown looked on. They were halfway down the hallway when Mathias suddenly paused in mid-step.

"Ms. Thompson?" he called without turning around.

Sundown quickly moved back into her room and shut the door, the draft from her quick retreat tingling against her skin. She then put her ear to the door, listening for the savage growls she'd come to loathe. Occasionally, she could hear a low cry in the distance, but she couldn't determine if it was friend or foe. She sat leaning against the door until the toll of the day's grief and the night's fear weighted her with insurmountable exhaustion. She then crawled into her bed and fell asleep awash in her own cold sweat.

Webb dodged to his left, missing the Whoop-Dinger's initial lunge. Gaining his balance, he jumped upright and backed down the hall, keeping the Whoop-Dinger in his sights.

"...Webb?" came a whimpering cry from behind him.

Webb turned to find Iggy standing rigidly in the shadows of the hallway with his teddy bear gripped firmly in both hands. "Iggy, run!" Webb implored, but Iggy did nothing but continue to cringe behind his bear. Webb's first thought was one of anger: *what was Iggy doing out here in the middle of the hallway?* Then Webb realized that like everyone else, Iggy had been attracted by the noise. Trouble was, unlike the others, he didn't know how to fight or run.

Webb looked to his left and saw another door. He quickly grasped for its handle and found it thankfully unlocked. In one fluid movement, he threw Iggy inside and slammed the door shut. He then turned his attentions back to the charging Whoop-Dinger.

"Hey, UGLY!" Webb screamed, ensuring that the creature's attentions were drawn away from poor Iggy waiting helplessly behind the closed door. The Whoop-Dinger quivered and let loose a menacing howl at Webb.

There was sudden motion to Webb's right and he rounded towards it, thinking another Whoop-Dinger was upon him, only to find an incensed Gustafson charging past with a toothy snarl. The Whoop-Dinger shrieked and scuttled away down the hallway. Gustafson, however, wasn't content with just scaring it away. Instead, the black Felidae pursued the monster into the deep darkness. Moments later, there echoed a shrill inhuman cry.

Webb tried to move to check on Iggy when another gurgling moan slithered to his ears from the darkness. Webb hesitated. The acoustics within the fortress walls made it difficult to tell where the creature was coming from. He paused only a moment longer before deciding the sound was coming from behind him. He haphazardly sprinted around a corner and smashed directly into Caleb.

The collision threw both boys hard to the ground. Webb was the first to right himself, although he wasn't certain of how many precious seconds had ticked away since the impact. He looked over and found Caleb stirring slowly. Instinctively, Webb grabbed him and started to steer the both of them away from the sound of the charging Whoop-Dinger, when suddenly the pitch changed. There were now two distinct growls, from two different directions. Webb's stomach lurched at the realization that they were surrounded.

Out of the corner of his eye, Webb saw the first Whoop-Dinger materialize from the darkness, glinting wetly under the light. Seconds later, the other one emerged before them. Caleb, still being supported by Webb, turned his head listlessly from side to side, as if trying to find an escape route that Webb couldn't see, but there was nowhere to run. He tried to lift his hand feebly in an attempt to disperse the creatures, but the hand fell weakly. Webb took a step back and was met by the hard surface of the corridor wall.

The creatures closed in, so close now that Webb could detect a foul ammonia-like stench coming from them. He clenched his teeth, hoping that the end would be merciful, even though what he'd seen previously appeared to be anything but that. Then, curiously, both Whoop-Dingers stopped their advance.

For what seemed an eternity, Webb and Caleb found themselves just inches from the Whoop-Dingers, the creatures' repugnant odors causing both to involuntarily gag. Just as the inexplicable standoff began to border on maddening, the monsters suddenly withdrew a few feet and began to sputter.

Their tremors were almost imperceptible at first, a slight ripple in their membranes. Then, the shivers became more defined, turning into outright spasms; it appeared as if the monsters were boiling from the inside out. Their translucent forms began to twitch and pop, a sizzling sound like water splashing on a hot pan hissing throughout the hallway. Webb and Caleb raised their hands over their faces in defense.

The sizzling suddenly intensified. One of the Whoop-Dingers shrieked out in agonizing pain, the other one soon joining in the chorus. The screams were louder than anything Webb or Caleb could have imagined. Both now moved their hands to their ears, but it took little edge off the cacophony before them. The creatures were violently shaking with grotesque jerks back and forth, their skins boiling in showers of steam as hot water popped forth randomly, shrinking the monstrosities down in the process.

Just as the screams reached a crescendo, the remnants of the Whoop-Dingers imploded and collapsed disgustingly to the floor with a burble. For a moment, Webb kept his hands over his ears, afraid that the symphony of terror would return. When he was certain it was all over, he slowly removed them and looked over to Caleb who was leaning groggily against the wall and staring down the hallway in front of them. Webb reluctantly followed Caleb's gaze, afraid of what he might see.

At the end of the hallway a lone figure stood in shadow, his arms by his side. For a moment, the figure just stood there immobile. It then stepped forward.

Both Webb and Caleb's mouths drew slack as Kane emerged from the darkness, his face hardened with anger. He seemed disinterested in them for the moment, more concerned about where the Whoop-Dingers had been instead. He ran his boot over the glistening remains of the creatures, sneering almost gleefully.

"I would suggest you both return to your rooms and lock your doors," he said very sharply, not bothering to look up at them.

"Iggy is a few doors back. We need to make sure he's okay first."

"He is fine, Mr. Thompson. Now, both of you, to your rooms," Kane replied impatiently.

Webb said nothing. Instead, leading along Caleb who was still dazed, he slowly moved away. They were several yards out when he turned his head back around and caught a glimpse of Kane still regarding the pooled remains of the Whoop-Dingers, his boot again grinding them viciously into the stone flooring. Without warning, he shot a look in Webb's direction. Webb quickly turned away, hoping that Kane had not seen him staring.

The boys moved without conversation down the hallway, the sounds of battle no longer echoing around them. Webb assumed that all of the Whoop-Dingers had by now been removed from Glorian, hopefully with as few casualties as possible. Webb's thoughts, however, were now consumed by a new problem.

He'd been wrestling with it since he'd first seen Caleb in the hallway, right before the Whoop-Dinger assault. Now, in the newly restored peace and silence, the thoughts rushed to the forefront of his consciousness. He looked over Caleb and tried to form a question, but Caleb beat him in initiating the conversation.

"Quite the evening," he said ironically. "Thanks for helping me out there."

"Yeah," replied Webb, finding his voice. He reached over and placed his hand on Caleb's shoulder, stopping him from walking further.

"What's up?" he asked.

"What were you doing in the hallway right before the Whoop-Dingers got through?"

"Just looking around like everybody else."

"But you were so far ahead of everyone else."

"So? You were ahead of everyone else too," Caleb replied defensively.

"I was trying to lock the doors back," he said. "I also was chasing the shadow of someone ahead of me, who probably was responsible for opening the doors in the first place."

Caleb furrowed his brow. "What's your point?"

It was the moment for Webb to unleash his allegations, but he couldn't bring himself to voice them. "...I just wanted to know if you saw anyone run by you. That's all."

"Well, you and then your uncle," he answered matter-of-factly.

"Thanks. Just wondering," Webb smiled half-heartedly. "I'll see you tomorrow then."

Caleb nodded and then slowly moved off.

Webb turned back around, his face fallen. The dark paranoid thoughts about Caleb would not recede. What was worse was that there was a strong logical progression to them. Caleb was the only one he knew to be so outspoken about his preference to stay in the Dark Lands, the only one who seemed to want to be here. Granted, Webb knew very few people in the Dark Lands, but Caleb's stance was just strange.

What if he'd been trying to guarantee himself an extended stay by ensuring that the balance of the Dark Lands was skewed—skewed because the Whoop-Dingers had eliminated some of the Glorians? And why had Caleb been alone in the hallway, suspiciously close to where the fortress had been unlocked? Had he been the shadow that Webb had seen fleeing the area? The one Webb so doggedly pursued because he was certain they had unlocked the doors? Mathias had said that two and two did not always make four, but this time it sure seemed like it did. Webb hoped he was wrong, but he had no way to prove or disprove it. All he had was the sickening feeling that he was right, but it was a feeling that wouldn't convince Mathias or anyone else. Voicing these suspicions without evidence would only result in another lecture about trust.

The doubts would not relent. They chased Webb all the way back to his room, hovering about his head like a low heavy cloud. When he reached his door, he took a deep breath and exhaled, his mind focused on temporarily removing the unsettling suspicions which unbalanced his thoughts. Almost instantly, Webb felt more at peace. The reservations about Caleb were still there, but they weren't as distressing.

The sharp tick of a cane clicking against stone further relieved Webb's anxiety. He'd recognize that sound anywhere and the corners of his mouth rose at the familiarity.

"Webb," Uncle Mike huffed out appreciably.

"Are you okay?" Webb asked, hastily coming to greet him.

"I'm always fine, my boy. It's you who I was concerned about, running here and there like you were."

"No need to worry about me, but what about Sundown? Is she okay?" Webb asked.

"She's just fine. Nothing made it to her side of Glorian; Mathias himself made certain of that," Michael said pointedly.

Webb let loose an audible whoosh of relief and then gave his uncle a brief hug. "Thank you for being there tonight."

"I think quite a few people did more than their fair share tonight," he winked.

Webb was too tired to appreciate the compliment and he instead just offered his uncle another exhausted smile.

"Go to bed, Webb. You've got another big day tomorrow. Hopefully not as exciting as today. Goodnight, Webb."

"Goodnight, Uncle Mike," Webb said as he turned back to his room, the sound of his uncle's tapping fading down the hallway behind him.

Webb opened the door, this time checking the bed and ceiling for Gustafson, but the big cat was nowhere to be found. Perhaps the Felidae was on patrol, making sure that the castle was safe. There was, however, something else sitting on his bed: a book.

Webb moved closer to it and noted a small piece of parchment atop the leather-bound tome. Written in very elegant handwriting was the following:

"Guess the whole day was a bad one. Thought this might end it right. Don't tell Mathias."

Webb moved the parchment aside and took a closer look at the heavy book beneath it. It was one of the Willkeeper's many meticulously-written volumes, but whose could it be? He picked it up and turned it in his hands to read the book's spine. A sudden rush, like the memory of summer days past, overtook him. *Daisy.*

Webb sat down on his bed, removed his shoes and changed out of his clothes which had gotten filthy from the day's ordeal. He then lay back on his pillow and opened the book, immediately absorbed by its prose. It wasn't just an account of his dog's life; it was as if Daisy herself had been able to recount her own life in her own words, moment by moment.

Webb was absorbed by each word, every sentence. He could see what she saw, feel what she felt; the tangibility of the words was amazing. He could feel the thrill of running wild, grass tickling at the soft pads of her paws. He experienced the pure joy she felt at playing in the park with them as a puppy, the lazy contentedness of sleeping on Webb's bed during the long winter evenings, the simple sadness she felt when she sensed the sorrow of the family in her last days. It was an experience that involved every facet, every emotion of Webb's being. It was wonderment incased, a vivid touch of magic from the Dark Lands.

When slumber finally wrestled Webb's eyes away from the book, his serene face and his pillow were wet with the tears of a dozen years of love and happiness.

And much later, when he was deep asleep, the book simply closed itself and drifted gently back to the Willkeeper's library. And no one was the wiser.

CHAPTER EIGHTEEN

A CHANGE OF SCENERY

When Webb awoke the next morning, his first instinct was to reach for Daisy's book, but all he found within his grasp was another piece of parchment paper. This one read, *"Time's up. Remember, it's our little secret."*

Webb grinned sleepily and stretched out, the tension from the night before slowly winding its way out of him. He pulled on his clothes for the day, this time an ensemble of worn jeans, ankle-high work boots, and a dark blue oxford with a t-shirt underneath. His mom had always called this his "frat-boy" look despite the fact that Webb was still in high school. The memory gave way to another sad pang, resonating somewhere between heartache and homesickness.

He shook off his worries about his parents and moved on to thoughts of breakfast, his mind quickly falling under the allure of soft sweet waffles and crispy bacon. Once again his nose registered their presence on his desk before his eyes actually saw the food sitting there. Guess he would be dining alone again this morning. He sat down, feeling a slight twinge of guilt at being such a recluse the past two days. Webb knew he should just go to the cafeteria and endure Sundown's angry glare long enough to get his apology out, but that would also mean he'd have to risk running into Caleb or Badego, and he just didn't know if he could get through the typical breakfast banter with them. Webb sighed at the quandary and took a bite of his bacon. Crispy and savory, the food was delicious as usual and temporarily took the edge off of his worries.

His eyes drifted around the room. Despite the otherwise fairly accurate replication of his bedroom, there were a few items conspicuously absent. Namely, there was no computer, television, or telephone. It was something he had noticed before, but he had not really appreciated it until this moment. He really wanted to watch some TV to relax for the moment, but modern technology didn't seem to exist in the Dark Lands—not even as spiritual manifestations. He wondered if he wished hard enough for a television or a radio, would one materialize? *No harm in trying*, he mused.

He closed his eyes, visualizing his television to the tiniest of perceivable details, from the individual little pixels on the screen to the dust clinging in the vent holes in the back. He thought and thought and thought. When he was certain he had done all the imagining and wishing that he could, Webb opened his eyes.

Nothing.

A look of disappointment spread across his face. *Well, you can't always get what you want.*

There was an abrupt knock at the door and Webb felt as if his heart had jumped into his throat. It was Kane for their second lesson. He looked down at his half-eaten breakfast and pushed it away, his appetite suddenly deserting him. He then made a weak attempt at getting out of his chair only to have the gravity in his mind reel him back.

It wasn't that he was afraid of training or sparring with him; he'd actually come to peace with that inevitability. Webb's fear was that Kane would be able to bore into his soul with his eyes somehow and know that Webb had seen him last night, had seen that moment when he was staring down upon the remains of the Whoop-Dingers, kicking and grinding them with his foot—with all that hate. What would Kane do when he realized that Webb had seen him in that state of such raw emotion?

He rose and reluctantly walked to the door, holding his breath as he opened it.

"Geez, Webb. Took you long enough."

Webb exhaled loudly. "Uncle Mike?"

"That's me," he said limping into the room.

"I just wasn't-"

"Expecting me?" he interrupted.

Webb nodded.

"You were expecting Kane, I would guess."

"Yeah," he responded uncomfortably. His uncle must have heard about their little tête-à-tête.

"Well, I will be your facilitator for today, not Kane," he said cheerfully.

"You?" Webb exclaimed loudly. "That's great!" Suddenly, his shoulders felt very light.

"It was Mathias' idea."

Webb looked puzzled.

"Come on, let's go," signaled his uncle.

Webb followed his Uncle Michael out of the room. This day was shaping up to be a good one. Moments later, they were outside, heading slightly askew from the hill where Webb and Kane had been the previous day. The air today was very sharp and chilly, nipping at Webb's ears and nose.

"Kind of cold this morning," Webb commented, shoving his hands in his pockets.

"The temperature, very much like the rains, adjusts for imbalances in the Dark Lands. It gets cold sometimes, but never much colder than this," Uncle Mike assured. "Well," he added, suddenly reconsidering, "there are certain places like the Passage of Oradour, but that is another story for another time."

Webb smiled. Yet another question to ask in the future. He turned back to make another comment to his uncle when he noticed that his limp was much more pronounced. He moved slowly and his cane supported more of his weight than usual.

"Your limp seems worse this morning."

"It hurts more on some days than others," he replied distantly.

"Memories?" Webb figured the stress of last night was what triggered the painful reminiscing.

"Yeah," he replied, pausing for a long moment.

"It was a rough night for everyone, huh?"

An uncomfortable silence ensued, one where Webb didn't know if he should say something else or let well enough alone. He chose the latter and waited for his uncle to say something, which he did after a few more moments of contemplation.

"Sometimes thinking about her and the way she died, it makes my heart ache. Every single day I look around and hope that she'll be here, but..."

Webb looked down. He was twelve when his Aunt Cathy had finally been overcome by the cancer. The many months leading up to it had been painful enough, watching a once vibrant lady waste away to literally a living skeleton. In the end, she had been so doped up on morphine that she could hardly even be construed as "living" anymore. Through it all, his uncle had never left her side. Even after she finally died and the hospice staff implored Michael to let her go, he had refused to do so, holding her head in his lap for several hours thereafter, just stroking her hair while warm tears ran freely down his cheeks.

"Webb?" Michael's voice sounded troubled, just barely audible over their brushy footfalls as they trudged through the dense grass.

"Yes?"

"How... how's my brother, your dad?"

The question caught Webb off-guard. It was so simple and innocent, and yet, so strange, things being as they were. Webb wondered if such questions were permissible in the Dark Lands.

"Don't worry, son. You can talk about it," his uncle added reassuringly.

"Uh, well, he's okay. He has his good days and his bad."

Uncle Mike nodded and smiled. "We were just so close. I know that if he had been the one who... died," he almost choked the word out, "...I would've had a real hard time."

Webb tried to think back to the circumstances around or aftermath of his uncle's death, but just as Mathias had promised, the recollection was hazy.

"It was tough for him," Webb improvised. He couldn't quite remember, but he had to say something. "But, you know, he... adjusted, I guess. You just have to adjust to... uh, stuff like that," Webb continued awkwardly, inwardly cringing after the words escaped his mouth. They had sounded so cold.

His uncle showed no displeasure. Instead, he gave Webb a firm pat to the back followed by a sincere, "Thank you."

"Sure," Webb responded, not knowing what else to say.

"You did very well last night, Webb. The Glorian Council was very impressed," he commented, changing the subject.

"I didn't really do anything, Uncle Mike."

"No, son, you did. When you heard the doors to Glorian prematurely unlocking, you didn't hide, you didn't wander curiously gawking around like so many of the others. You *reacted*, Webb. You reacted by trying to right the situation."

"Well, it had to be done."

"Exactly!" exclaimed his uncle. "You instinctively did what so many others here could not or would not do. You selflessly strove to protect the people of Glorian."

"I think I was more concerned about my own skin than anything else," Webb said meekly with a laugh.

"Is that so...?" smirked his uncle. "Then why did you ask me about Sundown? Why did you risk your own safety to get Iggy out of harm's way? Why did you help Caleb while the Whoop-Dingers were chasing you?"

Webb said nothing, his mind drifting to Caleb and wondering whether he should say anything to his uncle about his suspicions.

"You're a leader, Webb. The Council sees that. They've seen that in you since your deliverance here."

"How? Mathias and Kane are the only ones on the Council I've met. The others I've never even seen."

Uncle Michael slapped his knee and guffawed. "Just because you haven't seen them doesn't mean they haven't seen you!"

"Whatever," mumbled Webb dismissively. "But what happened last night, Uncle Mike? There's obviously a traitor here. Hasn't the Council realized that?" he asked, hoping to have a venue to air his suspicions.

"The Council is unsure. It could very well have been one of the Dark Man's manifestations that managed to slip into the compound. After all, no one witnessed who actually unlocked Glorian."

"What about the Willkeeper?" erupted Webb. "He knows everything!"

"Not if it was the Dark Man's doing he doesn't. The Dark Man can shroud himself, his followers, those in league with him, anything and everything-or so I have been told. So, even if it was a traitor, as you put it, someone would have had to witness the person doing it. Catch them in the act as it were."

Webb started to speak, but stopped himself, despite the burning he felt in his chest. After all, he'd only seen a slinking shadow. Nothing concrete.

"Nevertheless, it was something that has never happened before, so the Council is keeping a close eye on the situation, so to speak."

"Good. Last night was awful," Webb grumbled.

"That's why I'm facilitating you today. Mathias thought that you'd been through enough yesterday and a small reprieve might be in order. Now, I'm not as skilled as Kane, but I can get you on the right track. Depending on how things go, we might even move on to the classroom."

"With the rest of the Dispersers?" Webb asked.

"We'll see. Let's get to the lesson, shall we?"

"Let's do it!" replied Webb earnestly.

He greatly preferred the option to train with his uncle rather than Kane. After all, his uncle had been a teacher in life. That should make him a great facilitator.

Uncle Mike stopped walking and slowly looked over the landscape. "The overall concern with you, Webb, is that you've been able to engage your abilities only when angered."

Webb grimaced outwardly. "So I've been told here and there."

"But do you understand the concern?"

"Yeah, sort of," Webb said hesitantly.

"Which basically means 'no.' Let's make it short and sweet—something I know that Kane and Mathias aren't that good at."

Webb smiled at his uncle's attempt at levity.

"It is human nature to always follow the path of least resistance. Right now, it seems that the easiest path for you is to tap into your gift through anger. If that is indeed the case, then subconsciously you could end up being so connected with your anger that you'd eventually become predisposed to its influence. And that would play right into the hands of the Dark Man and his minions, you see?"

"Putting it that way, yeah."

"Anger can make you jealous, suspicious, and paranoid. It can make you a lot of things, almost all of them agents for the Vindicadives to act on. So, we work on tapping the right emotions." Uncle Mike reached into his pocket and pulled out a handful of red marbles.

"Where did you get those marbles from?"

"Your room just earlier this morning, when I came to get you," Uncle Mike replied matter-of-factly. "Guess you weren't paying too much attention." He handed the marbles over to Webb. "Now, take them and cup them between your hands."

"Here we go again," Webb muttered.

"Not quite. I want you to use your gift to make them swirl ever so lightly within your palms."

All Webb felt was the familiar swirling in his stomach over his impending failure. Disheartened, he looked into his hand and focused on the orbs, but nothing happened.

"Webb, you're trying *too* hard. Relax. Think how funny it will feel and sound when they start spinning."

Webb cleared his mind and again looked at his cupped hands. He began to think of a merry-go-round in a nearby park that he and Sundown used to frequent and how the glittery horses would shine in the sun as they moved. He transposed the image to the marbles and imagined how their glassy sheen would glimmer the same way as they spun and circled one another. Just then, his palms began to tickle and he heard a clacking sound. The marbles were moving. Peering between his closed fingers, he could just see a glint here and there as they swirled. Webb looked up at his grinning uncle.

"See Webb, being a Disperser is more than just knocking things around. It's about being able to use kinetic energies to move things, and to have those movements be defined and precise, not blunt and sporadic. It comes with practice and patience. The more you have of both, the more you will be able to channel your gift. That's why you'll appreciate the group settings. There, you can share your learning experience with others."

Webb nodded, but he hadn't heard a fair portion of what his uncle had said; he was so fascinated with the marbles ricocheting within his cupped fingers. The sensation had gone from gentle to intense, like the cycling of a washing machine, and Webb started laughing. The harder his laughter became, the faster the marbles began to move, as if they were in an interdependent connection with his emotions. His laughter became so great that Webb suddenly found it hard to stand, his knees buckling. The marbles went from simply tickling to maliciously biting. The pain surprised him and Webb's fingers flew open, the marbles exploding freely into the air.

Uncle Mike ducked as the red orbs thudded on the ground irregularly. He looked over to Webb and saw his nephew running after a wayward marble spilling down a nearby hill.

"Let it be, Webb. There are plenty more," he called out.

"Don't worry, I can get it," Webb said as he closed on the marble.

"Webb, *stop*!" His uncle shouted, a sudden edge to his voice.

Webb halted and looked back towards his uncle who was quickly hobbling towards him, his face panicked and arms waving wildly. Webb looked down and saw that the marble had suddenly picked up momentum and was rolling quickly towards a dark hole at the bottom of the hill, the grass too smooth to offer enough resistance to stop it. The hole was huge, a radius of at least seven feet, and Webb suspected that once the marble fell in, it would be almost impossible to find.

Ignoring his uncle's protests, Webb reestablished pursuit, certain that he could get to the marble before it was swallowed up. He was within a few yards of reaching it when his feet were abruptly knocked out from under him, tripping him hard into the ground face first.

He shook the jolt of the impact off and looked up at his uncle ambling down the hillside. "Did you just disperse me?" Webb asked as he got to his feet.

"YES!" his uncle roared in between heaved breaths.

Webb looked back at the hole, the marble now nowhere in sight. "What's your deal?" he asked as he took another step towards the small cave in the ground.

"Webb, stop! NOW!" his uncle roared, so violently this time that Webb froze on the spot.

"…Isn't it just a hole?" protested Webb.

"Not *just* a hole, a *veil hole*," he huffed as he reached the boy. "Approach it very cautiously."

"What's a veil hole?"

"Come with me," he said, leading Webb delicately to the edge of the opening. "Look down into it and tell me what you see."

If there was such a thing as liquid night, then that was what Webb saw. All the way around its perfect edges, there was nothing but abysmal darkness. The afternoon light offered no measure of vision into the unnatural gape. In fact, now that Webb had a chance to examine it closer, it was the most perfectly symmetrical hole he had ever seen, as if someone had taken a drill and bored straight through the fabric of reality.

"You see no bottom? No sides? Just darkness?"

"Yes."

His uncle reached into his pocket, retrieving another one of the red marbles. "Listen closely." With a grunt, he drew his arm back and threw the marble as hard as he could into the opening.

Webb leaned his head closer to the void, anticipating the sound of an impact or ricochet, but no sound ever surfaced to his ears. Carefully, he knelt down and looked deeper, his uncle's hand holding securely onto his shoulder. There was a definite chill to the chasm, frosting Webb's breath as he leaned over. He strained his eyes, but there was absolutely nothing to be seen but infinite emptiness. Webb plucked a blade of grass and began to move it towards the hole curiously, but his uncle jerked him back.

"That's enough. Let's move away now," he said firmly.

Webb brushed the grass from his hand and the two moved back up the hill. When they reached the top, Webb turned around and looked once more into the strange vortex.

"What is that again?"

"A veil hole, Webb. A hole that has no ending—a true bottomless pit."

"So, if I fell into that thing…"

"You'd fall forever."

Webb felt as if a cold hand had just slapped him. "Forever?"

His uncle nodded.

"Has anyone ever fallen in?"

"Several. Some by accident. …Some by malice."

"By malice, you mean that the Vindicadives did it?"

"Yes, veil holes can serve as ally and enemy."

"Can they suck you in? Like a black hole in space?"

"No. In that respect, they just are like normal holes in the ground. They cannot suck you in or grab you. They are what they are, where they are. You just stay away from them."

Webb went silent, visualizing what it must be like to fall forever. He imagined that there would initially be a funny sensation of floating within the stomach. The already sparse lighting from the skies over the Dark Lands would then be washed out by the ever-enveloping darkness as you fell deeper and deeper. After that, there would be nothing but weightlessness, the chilling blackness and the howling of the air as your body eternally tumbled through it. That was assuming that the sheer terror of what was happening hadn't already overwhelmed your senses. How long in that environment would it take before you went mad? How long until you were finally blessed with death? Would death even come?

"…Do you know how many people have fallen in?" Webb asked, feeling morose.

"I don't know, son. The Willkeeper is probably the only one who does know. There are veil holes scattered throughout the Dark Lands and they've been claiming victims since the beginning of time."

"So there could be people that have been falling for thousands of years?"

"*Longer*," Uncle Mike replied chillingly.

Webb tensed uncomfortably. It was the most horrible fate he could think of, even worse than being consumed by a Whoop-Dinger. His eyes began to blink nervously.

"Let's get away from here, Webb. We've places to go," said his uncle.

"Good idea," he replied, turning around and heading straight back to the safety of Glorian.

If he never saw another veil hole again it would be too soon.

CHAPTER NINETEEN

CLASS

Webb walked briskly, feeling the eerie yawn of the veil hole still haunting him, as if it were a great eye watching him from behind. By the time he reached Glorian, he was covered in a thin coat of sweat. He turned back to find his uncle hobbling along in the distance, the sight of which overwhelmed him with guilt.

Uncle Mike had tried to make some small talk along the way, but Webb hadn't been in the mood for chatting. When his uncle's attempts at conversation had fallen off, Webb had assumed that the man had just given up trying to talk to him. Now he realized that he'd simply outpaced his impaired uncle to the point where Webb couldn't have even heard his uncle's voice if he tried to speak.

Webb leaned against the fortified walls, feeling its rough bricks hard against his back. To distract himself until his uncle caught up to him, he rolled his head to the side and inspected the masonry closer, hoping it would pull his thoughts far away from his guilty conscience and the horrible concept of veil holes.

There was an almost ethereal quality about the stones and now he realized why. Ingrained within each stone were thousands of celestial crystal granules, each with a starry diamond-like sparkle about them. Webb rubbed his hand flat over the bricks; the granules in the stone held firm. He wondered if they were what gave Glorian its glowing radiance during the night.

"Finally decided to wait for the old man?" Uncle Mike's voice rang out over the grounds.

Webb turned, his face clearly showing his discomfiture. "I'm sorry, Uncle Mike. I just wanted to get away from that thing as quickly as possible. I had my mind elsewhere…"

"No explanation necessary, son."

Webb nodded, glad that his uncle wasn't offended. He had always been a patient and understanding man despite his robust and rugged exterior. Glancing at the large entry doors, his thoughts floated to the events last night. "Hey, Uncle Mike?"

"Yes, Webb?"

"When Glorian is locked down, when the key is fitted in the keyhole, what happens? Why does the whole place rumble so much?"

"That is Glorian closing in on itself."

"How about we try explaining that in plain English?"

Uncle Mike chuckled gently at the comment. "Fine. Think of Glorian right now as an open palm," he responded, holding out his hand. "This is as she is most of the time, enabling us all to come and go as we please. When we lock her down, the stones themselves slide over the various entryways, creating an impenetrable sanctuary," he said, balling his hand into a fist.

"So, these bricks," Webb said as he pounded firmly on the wall, "just melt over the doorway?"

"Pretty much."

"Impressive," was all Webb could manage. Every day he found something new here to amaze him.

"Enough chit chat for now. We need to get back inside. We've got a schedule to keep."

"What do you mean schedule?" Webb asked as he followed his uncle inside.

"Classroom time," he replied.

"Am I ready? I mean I thought that I had to have a bit more preparation," said Webb, slightly nervous.

Uncle Mike stopped and turned to Webb, placing his hands on the boy's shoulders. "Webb, the initial tutorial is just to orient you with your gift, give you a basic understanding of it. Granted, your session with Kane went slightly askew, but it served its purpose. Wouldn't you agree?"

Webb gave his uncle a less than enthusiastic nod.

"It served its purpose," his uncle affirmed. "Just like our brief session today served its purpose. You know your gift. You know how to utilize it and how not to utilize it. Now you move on to an environment where you can learn and grow with your peers," he encouraged.

"I just don't feel…"

"Ready? No one ever feels ready, Webb. Were you ready to die?"

The words made Webb flinch.

"That's another thing you've got to come to terms with, Webb, and I can't afford to be subtle about it," Uncle Mike said, his eyes boring deep into Webb's. "You are dead, son. Chances are you'll never see the living world again. I know you're put off by the way everyone appears so indifferent about being dead, but that's the way it is. Your world is here now. And what you're doing here and now, what *all* of us are doing here and now, I daresay is far more important than anything we ever did in the living world. Remember that."

His voice was frank, but not harsh, nevertheless the words still hurt. Webb's eyes glazed over suddenly as his uncle finished speaking, his tearful eyes sparkling like the walls around him. "I know…" he mumbled in a small voice. "It's hard, Unky, it's hard…" muttered Webb, slightly taking his uncle aback.

Michael hadn't heard his nephew call him "Unky" since the boy's tenth birthday. During that little coming of age celebration, after blowing out the candles, Webb had vowed to be like a "grownup," and he said that grownups didn't use childish nicknames like "Unky."

Webb's cheeks burned a little at first from the slip up, but then he realized that trivial embarrassments like those didn't matter anymore.

He had nothing to be ashamed about before his uncle, the man who was now gently reaching for his hand.

"I know it's hard now Webb, but in time, as with anything else, it will get better." His voice was softer now, more compassionate, and for a moment, it seemed to Webb as if they were back in the living world, sitting on the porch of his uncle's house, talking about random little things that, at the time, seemed so important to them.

Webb squeezed his uncle's hand, a squeeze that symbolized more than just a "thank you" for right then; it was a "thank you" meant to last a lifetime and beyond.

Uncle Mike nodded. "Let's move along then."

Webb tried to keep track of where they were going, but the hallways once again began to blend with one another. After a few more turns, they arrived at another nondescript door. Michael opened it, but instead of a room, there was a darkened passageway, a few hundred feet long, ramping up to a small point of light in the distance. He motioned Webb in and then followed suit, settling the door behind them.

Webb could just discern the steady drone of a man's low-pitched voice, familiar in its inflection, coming from the end of the tunnel. He tried to listen to what was being said, but the tunnel's acoustics precluded anything but the most rudimentary of muffles from reaching his ears over the sound of their own footfalls and the clack of his uncle's cane. The trek was short and soon Webb was at the top of the ramp, getting a first glimpse at his "classroom."

His initial impression was of a courtroom where old English barristers used to ply their trade in forensic debate. The room was oval in shape, its lighting consistent with the rest of Glorian: gloomy. Layers of dark acacia wood bleachers encircled the room, filled row upon row with Glorians of all ages and distinctions. Each row of seats was graduated one after the other, facing towards a large circular depression perfectly cratered at the room's center. And there within the circle stood Kane, adorned with his usual black trench coat and unpleasant scowl.

His had been the voice Webb had heard while traversing the passageway. Webb looked uncomfortably at the man and then, as if on cue, Kane glanced up and momentarily stopped lecturing.

"Ladies and gentlemen," said Kane, drawing each growled syllable out to its fullest extent. "Please direct your attention to the entrance and you'll find our newest *Disperser*."

Webb thought Kane had hissed the "s" sounds more than pronounced them.

"Some of you may already be somewhat familiar with Mr. Webb Thompson," Kane smiled mockingly into the stands. Webb looked over and saw that the sneer was aimed specifically at Caleb, making Webb feel all the more self-conscious. He didn't want to have to wrestle with his suspicions about Caleb right there and then, especially not with Kane leering at them.

"Regardless, I trust that everyone will do their part to help Mr. Thompson fit in and better develop his skill set."

Regardless? What was that supposed to mean? Webb scowled on the inside, but he didn't make any outward fuss with the whole class watching him. He couldn't believe someone as rude as Kane was even allowed to be *near* a classroom, much less be a teacher.

"Find a seat," Uncle Michael whispered into Webb's ear.

His uncle was right. Webb had been standing before the class, fidgeting around uncomfortably for too long. He needed to sit down before things got too weird. He nodded and looked around for a place to sit, glad to remove himself from the attentions of the room. Out of the corner of his eye, he saw Caleb eagerly signaling that the seat next to him was available, but Webb pretended not see him, opting instead for a seat at the end of a nearby front row bench, next to an cute red-haired lady. He sat down and looked directly at his feet, the awkwardness of being the "new guy" and the remorse of having snubbed Caleb both heightening his discomfort.

Webb didn't know how long Kane spoke. He did pick up a few words and a couple of disjointed sentences, but his mind was too wrought with the feeling that Caleb's eyes were burning holes in the back of his head. He knew that he should be listening more attentively, but the clutter of his mind was just turning everything into white noise. He started wishing for lunch or some other break just to be able to get out of the room and clear his head.

Suddenly, everyone in the room began to get up and shuffle about, moving towards the door and out into the tunnel with mumbling conversations. Webb stood up quickly, not wanting to seem out of place.

"Are you okay?" his uncle asked, angling his way through the crowd. "You seemed kinda out of it, kid."

"Yeah, I'm just tired," Webb lied.

"Well, just think up something extravagant for lunch," his uncle laughed as he passed on into the tunnel with the dozens of others Glorians. They were all hastily retreating to their rooms or to the cafeteria, eager to relax after the session with Kane. Webb began to file out with them but then stopped, overcome with the apprehension of running into Caleb.

He turned to see if Kane was still standing in the classroom, but he too had already gone. The room was now completely empty. The silence quickly became too much to bear and Webb moved down the tunnel and back into the main body of Glorian.

Caleb was waiting for him.

"Oh, hey, Caleb," Webb nodded, masking his face with a false smile.

"Why didn't you sit by me back there?" he questioned, nodding towards their class.

"I didn't see you," Webb replied awkwardly.

"Yes, you did. You looked right at me."

"Oh, I did?" Webb could think of nothing else to say.

"You know, you've been acting really strangely since last night."

Webb paused. "Fair enough, Caleb." He couldn't stomach another line of half-truths or lies—not from himself nor from Caleb. "I need to ask you something," he said.

"What?"

"Last night when the doors were unlocked and the Whoop-Dingers got in, I caught sight of someone running from the keyhole. I'm pretty certain that someone was responsible for what happened."

"You've told me that already," replied Caleb tiredly.

"Well, I chased after that someone and came upon *you*!"

A look of indignation came over Caleb's face. "Am I hearing you right? You think *I* opened the doors? Just because I was in the hallway?"

"Think about it, Caleb. I see someone running away and I chase them down only to find you alone in the middle of the hallway. And if memory serves, you did seem rather flustered and out of breath. Now what would you think if you were in *my* position?"

"I think *I* wouldn't be so eager to point fingers!" Caleb fired back.

"But you were the only person in the area!"

"What about your uncle?"

"Come on, Caleb! You've seen him hobbling around with his cane. The shadow I saw was in a dead sprint. Besides, my uncle was coming from the opposite direction, so it couldn't have been him. That means it was someone else and you were the only other person there. You said so yourself, remember? I asked if you'd seen anyone else and you said no."

"Just because I didn't see anyone else in the area doesn't mean that there wasn't!" he shouted.

"Fine, then what were you doing there, then?"

"I heard the sounds just like you. I ran to see what was happening."

"Then why did you look so out of sorts when I approached you?" Webb demanded, not bothering to hide the accusation in his voice.

"I… I don't know, Webb!" Caleb stuttered out. "I was there and then suddenly it seemed like I had just… lost time."

"Lost time?"

"There were a few seconds I couldn't account for, alright?! And to make it worse, I had a mammoth headache that came out of nowhere. Next thing I know, I'm talking to you."

"Oh come on! Do you know how ridiculous that sounds?"

"Ridiculous? Webb, look where we are! The rules of reality no longer apply."

"Don't use the Dark Lands as an excuse," Webb spat. "A person's nature doesn't change just because they're here. I've at least learned that."

"Oh?" Caleb's brow rose. "And what exactly do you propose is my *nature*, Webb?"

"You said you liked it here and didn't want to leave. You made that pretty clear. I think you might do anything to keep it that way."

"And that includes risking *my* life as well as the lives of everyone else in Glorian?"

Webb let his silence speak for him.

Caleb shook his head sadly. "I'm sorry you feel that way," he said as he brushed by Webb roughly, knocking him nearly off balance.

Webb couldn't make himself turn to call after Caleb or even watch after him as he disappeared down the hallway. If it was possible to feel even worse about everything, he did now. The ugliness of it all hung over him like a fog, immobilizing him until all he could do was stare ineffectually at the dusty stone below his feet. First Sundown and now Caleb. He was alienating himself rather quickly.

"…Webb?" called someone in the distance. It was a woman's voice.

Webb turned around to find Raven approaching him tentatively, apparently having caught the tail end of the argument between him and Caleb. Despite seeing how upset Webb was, she pressed on, though he could hear the hesitation in her leather-heeled footsteps.

"Yeah, Raven?"

"I can't seem to find Sundown."

He blinked and paused before replying. "What do you mean?"

"I haven't seen her since yesterday afternoon. She wasn't at breakfast. She didn't attend class this morning either. I'm sorry, Webb. I can't find her anywhere." Raven tugged at the ends of her silky black hair uneasily, the look in her worried eyes imploring him to say something to relieve her.

Webb momentarily felt sick. For a day that had started so promisingly, it had begun to grow dark very quickly.

CHAPTER TWENTY

WICKED PERSUASION

Tears streamed uncontrollably down Sundown's cheeks. The warm twin trails were a marked contrast with the cold around her. In a half-hearted attempt to shield herself, Sundown pulled her knees in tight against her body and wrapped her arms around them.

She had already been fragile before the night's Vindicadive attack, as Webb's words had been incessantly ringing in her head all day and night. The sudden attack had only served to wear her down more. She heard one man on Webb's side of the castle had even died in the attack. Everything was dark and frightening once again, just as things had been when they'd first arrive in the lands. It was dangerous; they could all die. *She* could die.

After managing to fall asleep, she had awoken from it all shortly to find herself no less distressed. Webb's accusations still stung her to tears as she tossed restlessly under her covers. It was the proof that she was only able to keep herself going by surrounding herself with pleasant memories, euphemisms and lies. Not reality. She couldn't accept their reality any better than Webb could. In fact, in many ways, she took it far worse.

Somewhere in this spiral of anguish, Sundown found herself running away from the suddenly claustrophobic confines of Glorian and into the open wilds of the Dark Lands. She couldn't recall exactly when she had left her room, but it didn't matter. In some bizarre way she felt she was free. She had run passionately, certain that her pain had given her the speed nearly matching that of a Muradian. She had run until she could run no further, finally collapsing in grief, heaving breathlessly and alone on an anonymous hillside, and that was where she had remained.

Sundown knew that time was passing by, but time had become meaningless to her. She knew that she'd missed breakfast and lunch and that the hour was fast closing upon evening, but none of it seemed to matter anymore.

She wiped her nose and then her eyes, her favorite pink windbreaker soaking up the moisture. Just thinking about the jacket only made her cry harder. It had been a gift from her mom, a simple gift from a carefree time when they had gone shopping together at the mall. She really couldn't recall much about that trip. Just walking around, browsing, and trying on clothes. All those mundane things didn't feel special then, but now represented a bygone moment. She had taken for granted all those times she and her mother had bonded as close friends and shared the innocent secrets of her approaching womanhood. Now she would never know what it was like to be a woman.

The sound of the breeze was joined by the soft footfalls of someone approaching. She felt no alarm, as these were not the steps of someone sneaking up on her to do her harm. These were the slow wearied steps of concern. Sundown's red, tear-soaked eyes looked up at the oncoming figure.

"Hello, Badego…" she sobbed out.

He stopped and gazed sadly upon her. "Hello, Sundown. May I sit down next to you?" he asked, gesturing towards her side.

Sundown nodded and sniffed.

He rested himself beside her, his fitted brown waistcoat bunching up underneath him as he did so. He gently took his arm and wrapped it around her. "What's all this, then?" Badego asked empathetically.

Sundown sniffed, unsure as to what she wanted to say, if anything.

"Come on now. We're friends. You can trust me," he implored, sensing Sundown's hesitance.

"But it might sound stupid to you," she sniffed.

"Cross my heart it will not," he swore, making the proverbial gesture of crossing his finger over his chest.

Sundown lifted her head off of Badego's shoulder and looked into his eyes sorrowfully. "I'm fourteen years old. And that's as old as I'll ever be," she sobbed.

Badego nodded gently.

Sundown wiped her eyes. "I'm never going to get older. I'm never going to have a life. I'll never fall in love. Never get married. Never have kids. Never watch them grow up in a house of my own. I was cheated out of my life before it ever began," she said between hysterical sobs.

Badego nodded and gave her another hug, this one much stronger than the last. "My dear, I've seen this same sadness many times in the Dark Lands and each time I find it just as heart-breaking."

"So, I'm not the only blubbering fool you've had to console?" Sundown asked.

"First, you're not a fool and, yes, I have seen many like you," he replied with a distant look in his eyes.

"But I'm the youngest, right?"

Badego nodded. "And it makes it that much more sorrowful."

"So you understand?"

Again, he just nodded, a melancholy look having overcome his face.

"And what makes it worse is that I'm crying over my own death!" Sundown shouted indignantly, the echoes of her words reverberating around them. "How crazy is that?!"

"And what brought all this distress about?" Badego asked gently.

Sundown sniffed again, followed by a stuttered exhalation. "I've... felt this way since I found out," she paused, fighting through a sob, "... since I found out I was dead."

"But then why are you crying now?"

"Doesn't really matter, does it?" Sundown mumbled and looked away.

"I had no idea," said Badego. "You seemed so happy to me."

"Yeah. I just hide my feelings. But I eventually break down and become totally useless."

"Not at all," Badego said with a laugh before suddenly becoming quite solemn.

Sundown noticed the sudden change in his mood and looked expectantly at him.

"I hesitate to say this, child, but I would feel remiss if I didn't tell you."

Sundown wiped her eyes. "Tell me what?"

Badego made a subtle glance around the area. "If I tell you this, I would be looked upon with disdain by the Council, as this is not something they want you, or anyone else, to know."

"What?" asked Sundown, curiosity superseding her unhappiness.

Again he made a cursory glance left and right as if fearful that someone was listening. "There is a way back to the living world," he whispered.

"I know. Resurrection or reincarnation," she replied despondently.

"No," he hissed. "There is another."

"What?"

Badego leaned in close to her. "Are you familiar with the Requiem?"

"Yes, my brother and I were there just two days ago. We were warned off by my uncle."

"And why did he warn you off?" Badego asked.

"Because the Requiem is a horrible place. It can turn you into a ghost or something."

An almost imperceptible grin spread across Badego's face. "For some, yes, but not for you. You are a Reclaimer, Sundown. The Requiem offers you a salvation not available to others."

"How?" she asked. "At best, isn't it just a window?"

"It is more than just a mere window." Badego looked deep into her eyes. "When you enter the Requiem, your life takes shape before you—a portal to your life as it was and as it will be. Most, unfortunately, are susceptible to the Requiem's seductions. Instead of *them* controlling *it*, *it* controls *them*."

"I know that much," she replied.

"A Reclaimer, on the other hand, can use her powers on the Requiem, forever altering her life's consequences."

"I don't understand."

"The Requiem exists in a realm between the living world and the Dark Lands," Badego said spreading his hands apart for emphasis. "What unravels before you when you stand within it is actually happening. It is not just a memory. *It is real!* And because of that, a Reclaimer can freeze it and rewind it."

"And change it?" gasped Sundown.

A knowing look spread across Badego's face. "Yes, you just need the focus—the will to change it. You could manipulate the time line so that you never died. And if you never died, then there is no way you could be *here*," he said, patting the grassy ground. "This paradox in the time line cannot stand, not even in the Dark Lands. Therefore, you'd be taken back into living world as if you'd never left it."

"But in the Requiem, aren't you just a ghostly observer of your life? How could you affect the time line?"

"True, you are an observer," Badego replied impatiently, "but you still are in flux between here and there. You've heard of poltergeists, haven't you? You still have some sway on events, whether it's as simple as making someone's comb fall on the floor or something as obvious as materializing before them. Such events can sway the hand of fate. After all, fate is but a matter of carefully placed events."

Sundown's eyes suddenly blazed, envisioning the possibilities. "So, the slightest thing I affect would change what happened to me, change what caused me to die and come here?"

Badego nodded. "I know it's hard to fathom and it can give you one dandy of a headache if you dwell on it too much, but it is true."

"You said the Glorian Council doesn't want people to know this. Why?"

Badego smiled apologetically. "They are old and set in their ways. They believe that if one comes here, then one is meant to stay here until other circumstances make it otherwise."

"And you don't?" Sundown asked.

"Not when it causes unwarranted pain."

Sundown shoved her hands back into the pockets of her windbreaker and stood. She looked towards Glorian shining in the distance. The way it glowed, it was like a white halo contrasting starkly against the black clouds beyond. "I don't know," she finally said.

Badego rose and smoothed his waistcoat. "What's *not* to know, Sundown? All that pain spinning inside of you? Don't let some misplaced loyalty skew your better judgment."

"Misplaced loyalty?" she replied, slightly disconcerted at the comment. "You've said that once before."

"Yes," he replied sullenly. "There are far too many here who believe their existence is better spent protecting Glorian than themselves. And that causes more problems than you could know."

Sundown began to feel uncomfortable and took a step back from Badego. "I don't know, Badego. I don't think I'm ready yet," she said nervously.

"Yes, *I think you are*," Badego hissed edgily. "*You want to go home.*"

Sundown suddenly felt overcome by the strangest of sensations, an enigmatic feeling of being bathed in pure expectant joy. Everything was going to be okay, she just knew it.

"Yes," she replied to Badego. "I want to go to the Requiem now."

The small gnawing in Webb's stomach had now grown into a ravenous tearing. He had tried several deep breaths to expel the pain, but it didn't help. Sundown was still missing and he feared that his outburst yesterday was more than likely the cause for her disappearance. He wished he could lessen the guilt by confiding in Raven, but his own conscience was enough of a burden right now. He didn't need Raven's judgment on top of all that.

"We've looked all over Glorian. She has to have gone outside. There's no other explanation," he said as he leaned breathlessly against a wall and slumped to the ground tiredly.

"Not necessarily," replied Raven.

"Raven, we've looked *everywhere*. No one is that good of a hider, especially not my sister," he replied, recalling how inept Sundown had always been at *hide and seek* when they were kids.

"You're still thinking in terms of the living-"

"Don't say it," groaned Webb. "I don't want to hear about how I'm still thinking in terms of the living world." He rubbed his hands over his face, trying to remove the exhaustion that was settling over him after running all over the castle.

Raven sighed sympathetically. "Do you know what your sister's gift is?" she asked, kneeling before him. The gorgeous ebony locks framing her face swayed as she did so.

"No," replied Webb, slightly uncomfortable that he was feeling attracted to Raven at such an inappropriate time. He averted his gaze from hers. "What is it?"

"She's a Reclaimer. She has the ability to rewind time around her. We could have come upon her dozens of times and she could have just manipulated the time lines so that it never happened. That's what I mean. So don't rule out the possibility that she isn't still within Glorian. Granted, she is a novice, but her skill level is such that she could have done it easily. Your sister, like you, is very advanced."

Webb ignored the compliment. "So, is that what you are? A Reclaimer?"

Raven nodded.

"Neat gift. All I can do is destroy things," Webb mumbled.

Raven placed her hand upon Webb's cheek. "Everyone's abilities have a purpose. Besides, only women can be Reclaimers."

"Kind of discriminatory isn't it?" Webb joked feebly.

"As it is such a dangerous gift, only the purest of souls can become a Reclaimer. And I have yet to encounter a *man* with a pure soul," she teased back.

"Well now that just sounds *really* discriminatory," he replied, rolling his eyes. "So..." he began, "you can just take time backwards whenever you want?"

"Something like that..."

"Good thing for correcting mistakes then," he replied good-naturedly.

"Yes it is," she said and then pulled close and kissed him.

Webb's eyes momentarily flew wide before sinking into the delirium of the embrace. He had kissed many girls before, but the passion of this kiss made all others evaporate from his memory. He was certain that there was a flow of electricity between and around them, encasing them in their own world. His knees grew weak and his heart felt like it would burst from his chest at any moment. He was enraptured and wanted never to know anything else. Then, just as abruptly, the kiss, and the spark ended.

Raven slowly withdrew from his widely staring face. "I'm sorry," she said as a tear slid down her cheek.

"…For what?" he asked. The words drooled out of his mouth more than he articulated them.

"For this." Then without further word, Raven drew time back, feeling ashamed of her licentious advance. Now was not the time nor place to explore her problematic feelings for this young man. Honestly, he was just a boy, but she'd been infatuated with him since his arrival, plagued with feelings she'd long thought had gone dormant. It was something she would have to address later—without the kiss. She had just needed to satiate her roiling emotions, and the intimacy provided a brief outlet for them. The sparkling tear rose from where it had hit the ground and Raven felt the warm caress of his lips once again, in reverse, and then the reclamation was over.

Another teardrop fell from Raven's eyes as she stopped time's recession. She wiped her eyes with the back of her hand and stared once again into Webb's eyes as time began its normal flow.

"Good thing for correcting mistakes," came Webb's voice again.

Raven nodded this time, unable to reply.

"What's wrong?" he asked, noting that her eyes seemed misty.

"Nothing. It's just that not all gifts are as wonderful as they seem," she said as she stood up and turned around.

Webb nodded blankly. The subtleness of Raven's comment had been lost on him. "So, what other gifts are there here?"

"Well, your *friend*, Badego, is an Influencer," Raven replied facetiously, trying to shake off the tugging at her heartstrings.

Webb rolled his eyes at the comment. "Sounds like a humble little gift."

"Hardly," Raven replied. "An Influencer can make people do things against their own will."

"Yeah. Probably only the weak-minded."

"No. Almost no one is resistant to an Influencer's suggestions. Naturally, Mathias, Kane and the rest of the Council are all immune."

Webb's jaw dropped. "Are you serious? Just the Council?"

"A few others, typically those who possess ridiculous willpower or overbearing personalities, like *yours*, can resist an Influencer's call," Raven jibed with a grin, "but it usually leaves a horrible headache in its wake."

Webb suddenly felt as if the breath had been sucked out of him. "...A headache?"

"Yes, a headache. It takes a monumental constitution to resist an Influencer, even if you don't realize you're resisting. Your essence does it naturally, but internally you endure a great struggle. It manifests itself in the form of a headache, and a terrible one at that."

Webb's mind began racing, recalling his confrontation with Badego and how his head had hurt so much when it was over. Then he thought back to what Caleb had said about having lost time and having a massive headache. "Can an Influencer make you forget things?" he quickly asked.

"Well, yes, to a point."

Webb sprang up, grabbing Raven's hand as he did so. "After an Influencer has affected you, are you confused, feeling like you've been in a daze or something? Maybe have a headache?" His voice was heightening, mounting in excitement, anger and fear all at once.

Raven looked startled at his transformation. "Well, from what I've been told, in some cases, yes. But why?" she asked guardedly.

"We've got to find Badego *immediately*. Chances are, my sister's with him." Webb turned and began racing towards the nearest set of doors leading to the outside.

"Webb, what are you talking about!?" pursued Raven.

He spun around and grabbed her by the shoulders, a fire burning in his hard set eyes. "Raven, *Badego* is the traitor! He's the one who unleashed the Whoop-Dingers on Glorian."

"*What*? Why!?" Raven gasped out. "He is one of us!"

"I don't know and right now I don't care. But I know he's got my sister."

"That is ridiculous!" Raven protested, shaking herself free of Webb's grasp.

"I know what I'm talking about," he replied. Without waiting for Raven to respond he turned down the hallway in a mad sprint.

"Webb, at least wait for Michael, or Mathias!" Raven called out pleadingly. If anyone could reason with Webb about the absurdities coming from his mouth, it would be his uncle or his mentor, but her pleas went unheard.

Webb was already gone.

— CHAPTER TWENTY-ONE —

FOCUS

Webb burst through the doors and out into the Dark Lands, the winds whistling around him as he ran. Every now and then, the whistling seemed more like a murmur, or a whisper trying to coax him this way or that. What it said, Webb couldn't really determine nor could he be certain that he really heard anything at all, but something triggered an inner voice telling him that it was time to listen to the Dark Lands and let it lead him to where he needed to go. From his few excursions outside he'd grown to mistrust anything in the wilds of the Dark Lands, but right now all the monsters and veil holes in the world didn't matter. He had to find Sundown before something terrible happened to her.

In full sprint, he ran past the huge fortifying walls of the fortress and there, grazing in the distance, were the Muradians, just as he had been counting on. They were the only realistic method he had for finding Sundown and returning her to Glorian before six o'clock fell, but taming one quickly enough might prove to be difficult. The last time he'd had Sundown's help. Now, he was alone.

Webb took in a deep breath. "PJ!" he called out.

The Muradians began to stir and whinny as they eyed him, the intruder in their herd, and suddenly from their ranks came forth a lone Muradian, its sleek black skin shining brightly despite the dreary skies. The great animal reached Webb within seconds, neighing and quickly halting its gallop. It stopped before Webb and gazed at him familiarly, its hot breath misting around him like a fog.

"PJ?" Webb smiled.

The Muradian whinnied softly and offered something that appeared to be the equivalent of a horse's nod.

Webb slowly approached the animal and laid his palm gently upon its face. "I need you to help me find Sundown," he pled into the Muradian's ear. "I think I know where she's going, but I can't get there without you."

PJ stepped back and then bowed, allowing Webb to climb upon his back. When Webb had settled himself, PJ rose and turned very deliberately towards the outstretched lands before them.

Webb felt his stomach churn as he grabbed hold of the Muradian's neck. "To the Requiem, PJ! As fast as you can!"

The wet fog licked at their skin as Badego guided Sundown deeper into the mist and towards the billowing pink haze. He was beginning to feel the weird sensation of familiarity that always signaled the Requiem's proximity. Sundown's exposure to the call didn't matter, but he couldn't afford its seductions himself. He had a task to do—one that would ensure the eternal harmony that he needed but Glorian could never provide.

"*We are almost there, Sundown. We are almost to your salvation. Everything will be made right,*" he soothed repetitively with each step.

Sundown responded with a blank grin, her eyes glazed over from the narcotic whispers of Badego's intoxicating tongue. To her, it was pure ecstasy to be here, as if she had drank a glassful of joy and it was now circulating throughout her. Nothing could be more perfect.

A few steps further and they were at the mouth of the Requiem. It yawned open with a stream of pinks tendrils that snapped and lulled out lazily at them before dissolving into the mist. Around Badego and Sundown glowed a pleasant warmth, the haunted land promising nothing but happiness to those fools who entered. Badego felt the temptation seize at him, nipping at his own heart, but he turned around and looked deep into the blissfully oblivious eyes of Sundown, refocusing on the goal at hand.

"Now, my princess," Badego whispered, *"We need to go into the Requiem, so you can go home, but I need you to do me a favor first."*

"Of course," she smiled. Why wouldn't she do something for this magnificent man—her best friend?

Badego smiled. *"Before we get you home, I need you to get another person home first."*

Sundown just continued to beam stupidly. "Yes, of course. Who is it?"

"He's a great man who, like you, left a lot of unfinished business in the living world. He needs to go back home and rectify that," Badego implored. *"He can't do this without your help. Will you help him, Sundown? Will you share your wonderful gift with your friends?"*

Sundown nodded absently.

Badego clutched her arm even tighter, fighting back his own trepidation. He looked back into the Requiem, its undulating haze mesmerizing him. He bit his lip and again shook away the sensation of the bewitching aura. Badego slowly moved Sundown in front of himself, positioning his hands on her shoulders. He then began to guide her forward—straight towards the rippling light.

"SUNDOWN!!"

The quiet, tranquil moment had been breached. Badego angrily whirled around. Within the swirling fog, he could just make out Webb sitting astride the unmistakable form of a Muradian.

"Well, if it's not the suspicious brother," announced Badego sardonically.

PJ knelt instinctively, allowing Webb to slide off and land beside him. Webb took a few cautious steps forward. "Move away, PJ."

The great animal complied, slowly moving itself out of the haze.

Webb could just make out his sister behind Badego. She was peeking out at him curiously, her face and body language reflecting deep confusion. Behind her, he saw the disturbing gray silhouettes of the withered, open-mouthed souls trapped within the Requiem, a sobering reminder of what was at stake.

Badego grabbed Sundown and thrust her between himself and Webb, as if she were a human shield. His face twisted itself into a snarl. The pearly white teeth which he had flashed so many times before in his ridiculous grins were now more like gleaming fangs. "*That's close enough, Webb. Back off!*" he spat.

"Let her go, Badego!" Webb cried. He felt his head again begin to pound, just as it had during his initial confrontation with Badego.

"Now why would I do a thing like that after all the trouble I've gone through to bring her here?" he asked mockingly. "I think you better *calm down*, Webb. You don't know anything about what's going on."

In defiance, Webb took another step closer, grimacing from the pain as he did.

"Yes, you are immune to my suggestions it seems, but your *sister* isn't," he warbled nastily as he looked maliciously towards Sundown. "You know, I could have a lot of *fun* with her before you could even get close to me." Badego plied his hand around Sundown's slender neck for emphasis.

His threat stopped Webb cold in his tracks. "Why are you doing this, Badego!?"

The man's eyes narrowed at the question. A sneer crossed his lips before he parted them to respond. "Tell me, Webb. In your short time here, haven't you grown tired of the all the questions with no answers?"

"That has nothing to do with right now," Webb fired back.

"I'll assume by your evasiveness that your answer is 'yes.' And you've only been here a few *days*," he growled. "Pathetic! I've been here much longer, Webb, and it has worn on me. I am done with the Dark Lands."

"Please, just let her go, Badego," Webb responded flatly. He inched forward once more and looked at Sundown, her eyes lulling back and forth in their sockets. "Sundown, wake up!" he called out again.

"The hero to the last," Badego mocked caustically, tightening his grip on the girl. "Such a wasted effort. You know, I once thought that I too could play the hero and make amends for my sins, make a difference

170

here in the afterlife. What folly that was. All I found here were endless empty answers and empty promises," Badego continued, "...until *he* came to me."

Webb felt the familiar chill creep up his spine. "You mean the Dark Man."

"Yes, the Dark Man gave to me what Glorian never could: the promise of a real future." The man's eyes blazed passionately as he continued. "How many times have you heard the *'everything happens for a reason'* spiel? Hmm? How many times have you been given a *riddle* in place of an *answer*? How many times have you wanted some kind of proof that everything would be okay, but were given nothing but a pat on the back?! Well, I have to put up with that garbage no longer. No longer do I serve that impotent Council. *The Dark Man is my future.*"

"So he's what made you turn traitor? *He's* what made you unleash the Whoop-Dingers on Glorian to kill innocent people?" Webb responded incredulously. "How could you hate us that much that you would do this to us!?"

"*Traitor?*" Badego scoffed. "Who is labeled as a traitor or a patriot is something that inevitably changes over time. But rest assured, I was not driven by anything as petty as hatred or vengeance when I let the Whoop-Dingers into the fortress. The purpose had simply been to serve as a distraction so that I could collect your sister and bring her here. My plan would have worked as well, had I not stumbled upon Caleb and Mathias policing the hallways."

Webb winced. It was confirmation that Caleb had been innocent after all—that he'd merely been in the wrong place at the wrong time. It made him all the more angry.

"Of course, that boy, Caleb was simple enough to subdue. The mere suggestion that I wasn't there, *that he hadn't seen me*, put him in quite the predicament for a spell. His stupid waltz down the hall was even enough to throw you off from my trail. Mathias got in the way after that, so I had no choice but to come back at a later opportunity. Ironically, it was *you* who gave me that opening,"

"Liar. I've already proven that you have no effect on me," he countered defiantly.

Badego chuckled mirthlessly. "Oh yes, you proved that yesterday when you wouldn't accede to my request to trust me. But I noticed that the headache my suggestion caused sure gave you a nasty disposition, didn't it? Enough to make you turn on your poor little sister. Enough to make her cry. *Enough to drive her to me.*"

The words were like a thunderclap, snapping Webb to see the full consequence of what he'd done. He'd let his anger open up a rift with his sister, the most important person in the world to him, which Badego had been able to exploit for his sick purposes. Despite the repeated warnings of so many, he'd let his anger act as his agent. However unwittingly it was, he had become an instrument for the Dark Man.

"And so, here we are," grinned Badego, delighting in Webb's discomfort. "How is your head feeling, by the way? About to explode?"

"I've had worse." Webb glared at the gloating man motionlessly, unable to do anything. He swallowed the lump in his throat and tried to at least come back at him. "So, what does your *master* want you to do?" he asked derisively.

Badego tensed at the remark at first, but quickly sloughed off the boy's juvenile insult. He then smirked and stepped backwards towards the Requiem's mouth with Sundown in his arms, pink tendrils caressing their bodies lovingly. "Your sister is going to take time back to when the Dark Man left the living world. She is then, with a little coaxing from myself of course, going to splinter the time line just enough to allow for the Dark Man's survival. This paradox shall port him back in the living world, thereby changing all of our destinies!"

The thickening miasma swimming around Badego and Sundown was beginning to change from soft pink to a harsh fiery red. The portal could sense the two fresh souls drifting towards its hungry mouth. Webb felt the frenzy building around them and knew that it was only a matter of moments before the Requiem would absorb them both.

"I don't know what the Dark Man promised you, Badego, but I know enough about him to guarantee that it is all a lie," Webb said, inching still closer.

"Your naivety is laughable, boy!" Badego shouted. "What does a child like you know? All you *think* you know are the convenient lies that Mathias and the rest of the Council tell you. Just think about it; whenever you get worried or upset, they just tell you to take a deep breath and feed you ice cream to shut you up. Or are you too gullible to see that?"

Webb bit his tongue, doubt shadowing his mind for the briefest second. Seeing his poor sister held in the disgusting man's hands, however, recalled his resolve. "No, Badego. All I see is a coward who manipulates people and kidnaps little girls."

Badego's burnished brown eyes looked almost sad for a moment before he smiled once more. "If you were smart, boy, you'd have joined me in my mission. The Dark Man has promised me an eternity beside him for aiding his return. A true promise! Something the senile Council fools could never do. I'll reign with the Dark Man in a realm of our own, and you and the rest of the Glorians can have whatever he will leave you."

"I don't *care* about what you or the Dark Man want! Join him, fine—just leave Sundown out of this!" Webb cried.

"My apologies, Webb," he said darkly, "but your sister is an unfortunate, but necessary sacrifice. However, you need not mourn for her. She will sleep forever in blissful ignorance as a sulker." Badego jerked towards the Requiem's flaring opening, violently tugging Sundown with him.

In that moment, the anger that was coiling throughout Webb's body dissipated, usurped by the love he had for his sister and his fear of losing her. He could see her innocent face, hear her infectious laughter. Everything within him was now concentrated down to the most basic of levels: he was her older brother and he would protect her at all costs.

Webb was suddenly consumed by a tunnel vision that reduced his view to just that of Badego, everything else becoming nothing more than a blur, partitioned off by darkness and silence. Webb shot his arm forward, just as he'd done when he'd impulsively attacked Kane, but this time the feeling was different. He wasn't trying to attack Badego; he was saving his sister.

An electrical sensation began at opposite ends of his person and then ripped through him, converging at his core before surging forth like a lightning bolt from his extended arm, directly at Badego. The pointed impact struck Badego in the shoulder and wrenched him off the ground, tearing Sundown from his grasp, and raggedly flinging him, arms flailing, deep into the Requiem. He didn't even have the chance to cry out. Carried on wave after wave of raw, pulsating energy, the man found himself deeper and deeper in the blood-red haze until he could see nothing but the undulating specter of light and shadow around him.

A subsequent eerie silence settled around Webb and he became aware of his sister kneeling on the ground just ahead of him, still swaying awkwardly to and fro, unaware as to what had just transpired. Webb raced forward and grabbed her, fearing that at any moment, Badego would come charging back out at them, but nothing emerged from the Requiem save for the snaking tendrils still licking and popping ravenously, sensing their presence. Webb knew he should just grab Sundown and be gone from the wicked place, but he had to know what happened. He had to see it for himself to be sure. Fearfully, he leaned forward and peered into beautiful carmine insanity of the Requiem.

Webb could just make out Badego's silhouette in the depths, his face contorted in an expression of overwhelming awe, eyes frighteningly open wide and staring out. He was mouthing something frantically, flecks of spittle catching in his brushy moustache, but his insane blubbering ecstasy and the thick boiling fog made for none of the words to be discernible. Badego then began to stumble around and grasp at things, at phantoms which apparently only he could behold. The misty coils that had been licking in and out of the Requiem's entrance were starting to encircle Badego, tightening around his torso and limbs like pythons, making his movements jerky and sluggish, as if he were wading through a thick pudding.

Barely containing his disgust, Webb watched as Badego's body suddenly began to metamorphose from that of a strong young man to an aged grizzled specter, mummified by the dozens of obscenely probing tendrils. Badego, terrified, was now only able to move his mouth as it opened and closed in a barrage of garbled and unintelligible sound. Around him, the other specters began to materialize, each of them with a gaping maw no different from the other. Webb glanced from horror to horror, and when he looked back to Badego he found that he could no longer tell the man's newly mummified form from the older, more ancient ones.

Webb turned sickly from the *dance macabre* and slowly began to move away with Sundown cradled in his arms. The pounding in his head was still going strong, a parting gift from Badego, but Webb continued to plod forward until he was well out of influence from the Requiem's song. When he was completely free of the danger, he took a deep breath and exhaled the pain.

"PJ," he croaked. "I need you."

The sound of the Muradian's hooves thumping on the soft grass erupted immediately from the cool white mist, the animal's form coming into sight soon after. Webb gently set Sundown on the ground and held her still face.

"Sundown," he beckoned. "Sundown." He choked back the emotion that was beginning to swell within him. This was how it had all begun, calling to his sister as she lay prone on the ground. But now, she lay before him injured due to his own actions.

Sundown slowly began to stir, her eyes blinking away the glassy glaze that coated them. She looked at Webb in perplexity before her face fell in realization of what had occurred. He put his arms around her in relief and apology; she put hers around him in relief and gratitude. And there, in the middle of the Dark Lands, an embrace said what so many words could not.

"We've got to get back to Glorian," Webb said, wiping the tears from his sister's eyes. "Six o'clock is nearly here."

Sundown nodded and supported herself by hanging onto one of PJ's legs to stand. She felt stiff and weak, but the aches and knots loosened up as she steadied herself. Out of the corner of her eye, she caught sight of something amiss. There in the distance, holding court over the deserted landscape stood alone black figure. She recoiled with a small gasp.

Webb turned. His eyes were immediately drawn to the same figure in the distance—a shadowy form swallowed up by black robes flowing ominously in the breeze. He felt a sudden whisper of evil.

The Dark Man was here.

— CHAPTER TWENTY-TWO —

THE DARK MAN

The air around Webb and Sundown became permeated with a deep chill, their breaths becoming heavier and condensed in the mist. Webb slowly placed his fingers around Sundown's arms and moved her behind him protectively, next to PJ who nervously whinnied and shuffled his hooves.

The Dark Man stood arrogantly and unflinching, daring an intrusion by the children. Webb strained his eyes at the figure, trying to look past the hood and robes, into the untold evil underneath, but he could see nothing.

Webb knew that he should be afraid, but fear wasn't what was coursing through him. Instead, there was a pure and defined rage. Before him stood the root of all the tribulation in the Dark Lands, the evil that had tried to take his sister—and it was taunting them.

Webb's blood began to burn and he reactively threw his arm out, channeling the wrath, volleying forth a shock wave with such force that Webb was thrown to the ground in its wake. He righted himself in a scramble, watching in awe as his upsurge violently cut through the surrounding mist and rumbled towards the Dark Man.

"Webb, what did you do?" he heard Sundown gasp, but he didn't answer. He just kept his eyes fixed on the impending collision, his breaths faster in anticipation.

The billowing wave reached the Dark Man and then, with a sound reminiscent of a droplet of rain falling into a pond, it disseminated to nothingness. Webb's mouth went agape.

The Dark Man slowly knelt down upon the grass, his gaze upon them never wavering. Underneath the man's concealing hood, Webb could perceive a low cackling and feel the eerie prickling on his skin from an unseen aberrant smile. The malignant figure then deftly cleft the ground before him with the first two fingers of his left hand. There was a low rumble, much like a growl coming from the earth, and then the spot began to glow.

It began as a soft ember red, but then quickly crackled into a brightly burning yellow flame, deep orange fissures erupting from within them. The fiery chasm spread away from the Dark Man's touch, over the grounds, and rushed towards Webb and Sundown.

Sundown grasped Webb's arm. "What's happening!?"

"He's burning everything!" Webb replied as he watched the inferno blaze forward like a quickened lava flow. "PJ!" he cried out. The Muradian immediately lowered himself to allow for Webb and Sundown to climb onto his back. Webb got on first and then pulled Sundown up behind him. Her arms firmly encircled his waist. PJ did not need to be told what to do; he whirled and sped away in the direction of Glorian.

Sundown glanced around and saw that the Dark Man's firestorm was growing behind them, relentlessly enveloping everything in its wake. Yet, just past the fire's initial surge, the grass was already beginning to rejuvenate itself, creating a weird spectrum of lush greens and reds. They, however, were not as resilient as the Dark Lands. If the fire overtook them, they would be killed. She hung on tighter to her brother and closed her eyes as the wind whipped her hair.

The Muradian was reaching speeds that Webb could never have imagined. The scenery before them had blended together like an oversaturated watercolor. Everything was a blur. Despite the incredible speed they were hurtling at, the fire was still closing in on them; he could already feel the fire's warm breath on the nape of his neck. Soon, it would be nipping at PJ's hooves and then it would be engulfing them all together. If they could just make it to Glorian…

PJ began to slow inexplicably and Webb looked to see what had happened. His heart sank. Before them was an incredible veil hole, much larger than the one he'd encountered with his uncle.

"Webb, why are we stopping!?" Sundown screamed.

"It's a veil hole," he replied hopelessly. "We're trapped."

Sundown looked over her shoulder at the black circle sinking eternally before them. Raven had discussed these aberrations with her, but Sundown had never seen one for herself. Her mind was racing as to how it could be used to save them and she came to the inescapable conclusion. It was a great risk, but it was the only alternative they had.

"Send PJ into the hole!" she cried out as the flames began to draw closer.

"I'd rather burn!" Webb shouted over the incendiary roar behind them.

Sundown heard the chilling resolution in her brother's voice and knew she had to be the one to act. "PJ! Jump into the hole!" she ordered.

Webb opened his mouth to defy the command, but his words were cut short by a sudden uprising in his stomach, a flutter that signified the feeling of a free-fall. PJ had plunged them all into the veil hole.

Webb's first sensation was one of being smothered by a sheer blanket of ice. The air howled in his ears as he fell deeper into the abyss. He looked up and saw the gray skies falling upward. He thought he could make out a few fingers of the Dark Man's deadly fire licking at the edges of the hole, but they quickly disappeared and all became black. He felt himself breaking loose from his grip on PJ's neck and he began tumbling. *This was the first moment of what would be his eternity*, his thoughts numbly repeated over and over in his head. *This is it. This is the rest of my life.*

Sundown felt her brother spiral away from PJ and instinctively reached out to grab him, but missed, and in doing so, found herself flailing away from the Muradian. She clenched her teeth to fight back the urge to scream. Instead, she focused on the diminishing light above, now no larger than a pinhead. Concentrating on that point of light, she found her focus and everything went quiet. The howling stopped. The cold evaporated. There was nothing but her.

The backwards march began and the surrealness of reclaiming time once again overcame Sundown. She felt herself being pulled upwards along with Webb, and back onto PJ. Her stomach became nauseated as they emerged from the veil hole and returned to the greens of the Dark Lands with the fire at their backs, but Sundown powered through the fear and dizziness, her focus never wavering. They rode backwards towards the receding flames and then dismounted. Moments later, Webb's shock wave came cascading back into his open hand and returned into his person. She let the seconds tick back even further, ensuring that she would have the necessary cushion of time, and then she willed the recession to stop.

Sundown shook her head, clearing the disorientation. She found Webb standing before her and found him transfixed once again on the Dark Man, his arm preparing to strike.

"NO!" she shouted, latching onto his arm.

Webb turned angrily towards her. "Let go, Sundown! What's wrong with you?" he yelled, shaking her free of his arm.

"No, Webb. No!" she repeated. "You're no match for what he can do. I'm not sure what you're thinking right now, but nothing good will come of this."

Webb's gaze didn't move and neither did his arm, still locked towards the Dark Man.

Sundown stormed in front of Webb, standing directly in the way of his open palm. "Do you know what my gift is, Webb?"

Webb's narrowed eyes lifted from their angry haze and he nodded, the ire disappearing as he watched the tears well in Sundown's eyes.

"Then listen to me," she beseeched. "Nothing good will come of this."

Webb lowered his arm as she asked, but his gaze returned once again to the Dark Man standing immobile in the distance.

"Please," she said softly.

Webb felt the last of his resistance ebb as Sundown's pleas pulled him from his swirling feelings of hatred. The Dark Man would have to wait another day. Sundown was saved and that was all that mattered. He nodded to his little sister. "Let's go home, Sunny."

She smiled. "PJ, let's go home."

They both mounted the great animal and rode back towards Glorian.

The Dark Man kept his haunting gaze fixed upon them as they disappeared over the horizon. He then turned and slowly stalked back towards his shadowy kingdom, trailing his fluttering robes behind him. There would be another time. He had seen what he needed for now.

PJ moved expeditiously over the rolling grounds, his movements reflecting his urgency in getting Webb and Sundown safely back behind the castle walls. He knew that the dark hour was soon upon them. Webb held onto the Muradian's neck while Sundown sat pressed against her brother's back. He lazily watched as the landscape rose and fell indiscriminately as they traversed the verdant hills.

Four riders on Muradians suddenly bounded out of the ravine in front of them startling the tranquility. He immediately recognized Raven despite the fact that she was in the rear of the group. The remaining three riders were Uncle Mike, Mathias, and Kane. He nudged his sister. "Sundown, look."

"Webb! Sunny!" their uncle shouted as he broke from the pack.

"Unky!" Sundown called back. Webb slowed PJ to a trot as Uncle Mike came racing up.

Their uncle's face was flushed red with anger, but he was smiling weakly in relief. "What got into you, Webb!? Are you crazy!?" he screamed. "You don't go tearing out into the Dark Lands unattended, boy! Especially not when dusk is about to fall!"

"Uncle Mike, he came after me," Sundown interrupted. "If he hadn't, I would have been..." she let it trail off, visions of Badego's consumption by the Requiem overtaking her. Even in her near-comatose state, she had been aware of what had befallen him.

"What?"

"Badego tried to drag her into the Requiem," Webb answered, looking over at other three riders as they saddled up behind Michael.

"But why?" Raven asked.

"Because he was in league with the Dark Man," Mathias announced, causing all heads to turn towards him.

"You *knew*?" Webb asked accusatorily.

"Suspected." Mathias paused and turned his eyes towards Sundown. "Last night, when he came running over to your quarters, I found his motives for doing so puzzling. I'm sorry that I said nothing to you then, but I had no proof. Apparently, my suspicions were not unfounded and I do apologize for my inaction," he offered somberly.

"Apologize for your inaction…? That's it!?" Webb interjected sharply. "I think you owe us a little more than that!"

"But what good would dragging Sundown into the Requiem do for him, much less the Dark Man?" Uncle Mike interrupted, ignoring his nephew's brashness.

"I think it better that we discuss this within Glorian," replied Mathias as he nodded at the darkening skies.

"Good idea," intoned Kane. "Let's get moving." He held his Muradian still until everyone had ridden past him and then took up position in the rear.

They rode back in silence, Mathias leading and Kane guarding their flank. Minutes later, they had all dismounted and were within the protection of the castle. The familiar hum of the fortress doors grinding shut was a great symphony to the ears of Webb and Sundown. Mathias signaled everyone to his room to rest and calm down while he and Kane rounded the opposite corridor and disappeared from sight.

The two men walked silently side by side, their minds ablaze with the events of the day. They kept their troubling thoughts to themselves as they headed to a new large door set deeply in the thick stone wall. Without a sound, the door whisked itself open and enveloped both Kane and Mathias before inaudibly closing into the brick wall and disappearing once again.

The room inside was misty with a delicate low-hanging fog. An orb in the ceiling, the solitary light in the room, lit the mist as it danced about in the drafty air currents. Centered underneath the light was an arched stone bench of which behind it were seven high-backed chairs, two of which were empty. The other five chairs seated figures whose features remained indiscernible under the sparse lighting.

"This is not good, Mathias," stated the center figure.

"That is an understatement, Hays," replied Mathias as he moved deeper into the room with Kane following silently behind him. "We are in new territory."

"And what do you propose?"

"What *can* I propose? We must wait and see what *his* next move is. It is our only viable course of action."

Those at the bench stirred uncomfortably, but no one spoke in dissent. Kane motioned to say something, but immediately second-guessed his statement and stayed his voice.

"And what to do with the boy?" asked Hays.

Mathias sighed. He had known this question was coming. "I suppose you want to propose a *locking*?"

"Despite his bravery, the boy has brought some rather negative emotions with him—emotions which I don't believe we can wrest from his soul. He is unruly, unpredictable, chaotic. Given the increasingly complicated situation that is unfolding, a locking might be for the best. Even if only for a short while," Hays responded stoically.

"Kane," called Mathias, turning to look at him. "This decision will affect you as well. We'd appreciate your thoughts on the matter."

"I think you should ask *her*," Kane said as he motioned towards an older woman at the far end of the bench. "It affects her much more greatly than it does me. After all, she is the one who knows what is to come."

The older woman nodded almost imperceptibly.

"...If the time line indeed is trending that way," Kane added solemnly.

."My answer would be a firm *no* then," spoke the woman staunchly.

"Some might say you are biased on this matter," spoke Hays.

"If anything I am the one who is open on this matter. If the timelines continue as I remember then this will not bode well for Webb–or myself."

"But locking him would protect–"

"You have my answer, Hays," interrupted the older woman. "In my opinion, it would protect *nothing*." She gazed sadly towards Kane who, for his part, only looked indifferently at the ground. "What is to happen will happen. Trying to outthink the time continuum is reckless and more often than not, has devastating results."

Hays looked over the remaining seated figures. "It takes five votes to proceed with a locking. Let us see where we stand. Who votes for a locking of Webb Owen Thompson?"

Four hands shot up immediately, the woman being the only abstainer of the Council members seated.

Hays nodded and looked down to where Mathias and Kane stood. "We now need your votes. Do we lock Mr. Thompson or not? We need only one more assent to proceed."

From the misty shadows, Mathias could feel the man's disapproving gaze. "Mathias, do I need to ask where you stand?" Hays finally asked.

Mathias shook his head. "I think his locking would be a great mistake. I vote no."

"And Kane, where do you stand?"

They found the door to Mathias' study already open, the fragrant smell of freshly baked chocolate chip cookies guiding them inside the large oval chamber where an enormous plate awaited them. The comforting room, indeed.

Sundown quickly moved to the table hosting the cookies and sat down, pulling three large ones from the overflowing plate and biting into them as a triple stacked sugary sandwich. Raven took the seat next to her while her charge ravenously shoveled the remainder of one of the cookies into her mouth and subsequently gulped it down with a large cool glass of ginger milk. Sundown had never felt so hungry in all her life. She looked at Webb, who had taken the seat opposite her, and saw that his appetite was just as voracious.

Webb hadn't initially felt hungry, but the smell of the warm cookies overcame him. Now it was like an out of body experience as he watched himself take one, then two, then three cookies and devour them greedily. He was reaching for his fourth when he noticed that aside from his sister, he was the only one eating. Raven and Uncle Mike had not indulged themselves at all.

"Please, eat as much as you want. You've both been drained by your harrowing experience," rang out Mathias' dulcet tones as he entered the room.

Sundown reached for another cookie while Webb took the moment to enjoy a large gulp of ginger milk as well, its refreshing coolness shaking off his fatigue and making him feel revitalized.

Mathias took his seat at the head of the table while Uncle Mike elected to sit alongside Webb. Kane, who had walked in just after Mathias, opted to stand by the other desk, askew from everyone else.

Mathias folded his hands together. "We must briefly discuss the events that occurred here this evening," he said in concern.

Uncle Mike looked towards Webb, traces of mixed pride and irritation in his expression. Webb did his best to look at Mathias and not meet the gaze of his glaring uncle.

"Webb, your recklessness could have cost not only your own life, but that of your sister's—perhaps even more," Mathias said, his tone still neutral.

"What are you saying, Mathias!? I got there just in time! Any later, then she would have become part of the Requiem, doing what the Dark Man wanted!" Webb argued.

"Which was what!?" Uncle Mike exploded. "What exactly did he want with her?"

"To run time backwards of course," Mathias answered, raising his hand and silencing the room's stirrings. "Because the Requiem is a link between the Dark Lands and the living world, some believe that if a Reclaimer were to engage the Requiem and draw time backwards, she could manipulate circumstances in the living world as well as in the Dark Lands."

"Exactly," Webb interrupted. "Badego said the Dark Man wanted to go back to living world."

"He also said that I could resurrect myself through the Requiem," came Sundown's small voice, turning all heads towards her.

"I'm afraid that neither is a possibility," Mathias replied adamantly. "The Requiem's pull is just too strong to allow for anything of the like to transpire."

Sundown lowered her head in shame. Badego's manipulations aside, she had wanted to believe that she had found a way home.

"Without belaboring the point further Webb, you will never do anything as rash as today again. You will consult the Glorian Council on all future concerns," said Mathias decidedly.

"If I'd waited to consult you, Mathias, then it would have been too late. She would have already been gone," Webb protested.

"Webb, do you think that all the Glorian Council consists of is a troupe of senile old men drooling and wandering around aimlessly in their chamber gowns?" Mathias asked with an amused smile.

"Well, no," Webb replied, slightly disconcerted.

"Then rest assured that we have our ways of righting a wrong," Mathias said, arching one eyebrow as he did so. "Now, I think it is time we adjourn. It's been a busy day, more for some than others. Everyone needs a good respite this evening."

"Let's talk," Raven said to Sundown as she rose from her seat. Sundown nodded silently in reply.

Mathias then stood from the table. "Webb, I would like to speak with you privately for a moment before you take your leave."

Everyone got the message and filed out as Webb sat still at the table, feeling more uncomfortable as each person left the room.

"Webb," Mathias began when the door to his room had been shut, "I want to tell you that despite the rashness of your actions, I am very proud of the bravery and selflessness you displayed. You are beginning to show yourself as the true leader that I expect you will be."

Webb hadn't anticipated the praise and it caught him off guard. "Oh, thanks," he managed dumbly.

"That being said, you have still greatly displeased the Council. Kane and I conferred briefly with them to discuss that very matter. Your impulsive emotional decisions are too easy for the Dark Man to predict and manipulate for his devices; as you are now, you are a liability to all of Glorian. Subjecting you to a locking was proposed."

"What's a locking?" Webb asked, alarmed.

"Something you will not have to worry about for now. It takes five votes to warrant such an action and there were only four."

Webb exhaled. Whatever a "locking" was, he was glad he'd been spared. "That's good to know."

"I said *for now*. If you continue to ignore instruction, then you may find yourself short of a necessary vote. Now that the point has hopefully been made, I've one other thing I wish to discuss with you." Mathias took in a deep, healthy breath and then slowly exhaled while he gently massaged his bearded chin. "You look disdainfully upon me and the rest of the Council for not being able to stop Badego. Yes?"

"That's not true, Mathias," Webb objected. "I never said that-"

"But your tone and your mannerisms," interrupted Mathias, "said otherwise."

Webb sighed in surrender.

"Don't feel bad. I am not lecturing you about your opinion of the Council. Rather, Webb, I am trying to make you appreciate something about human nature. During your time with Badego, out there in the Requiem, did he attempt to justify his actions to you?"

"Yes!" Webb erupted. "Yes, he did!"

Mathias nodded knowingly. "As I would expect. And therein lies the real problem."

"What real problem?"

"That evil doesn't always know that it is evil, Webb. In fact, I daresay that most of the time, wrongdoers think their actions are justified. Very few start down a path with ill intentions. They start down the path wanting to do the right thing, for themselves or even for others."

"I find it difficult to believe that Badego thought he was doing the right thing by throwing my sister into the Requiem."

"In his own twisted mind, yes, he thought he was in the right."

"But he knew that he was working with the Dark Man," Webb protested. "People got hurt from his actions."

"Sometimes we only see what we want to see." Mathias smiled. "Just as you saw him as untrustworthy, but we did not."

"And I was right."

"But was that because you had some knowledge that the Council did not? Or was that because of some personal prejudice? Perhaps because you were being an overprotective big brother? Perhaps, if I may borrow a phrase from your generation, he just *rubbed you the wrong way?*"

"That wasn't it at all!" declared Webb.

"Oh, so you did have some knowledge that the Council was not privy to. Please enlighten me then, so that I might enlighten the rest of the Council members," replied Mathias humorously.

Webb said nothing at this challenge; instead he looked away and wondered why the table was now feeling so rough under his resting elbows.

Mathias nodded. "If you let them, emotions can allow you to feel anything is justified. It is, unfortunately, not always black and white. You think the Council is inept for not realizing Badego's treachery— and maybe we were. But were you any less guilty for letting your emotions paint Badego in an untrustworthy light?"

"But you've told me to let the Dark Lands guide me," replied Webb tiredly.

"As well I have. *The Dark Lands*, Webb. Not your emotions." Mathias stood and patted Webb on his back. "Remember that. Come now. Before you go, there is someone else who'd like a small word with you as well."

Webb's shoulders drooped in anticipation of another lecture. From who though? Hadn't the entire gamut been run already, or did Kane want to get his licks in as well?

Webb heard the light footfalls behind him and turned to find Iggy beaming at him, teddy bear firmly in hand. A smile spread immediately across his own face although he didn't know if it was due more to Iggy's joyful presence or the fact that another reprimand was not coming.

"Usually, one of the Council members keeps watch over Iggy, but he got away from us during last night's confusion. I'm afraid his curiosity can lead him to dangerous ground at times," Mathias said, putting his arm affectionately around him. "None the less, your selflessness kept him out of harm's way and I, as well as *all* of the Glorian Council, want to thank you for that."

Webb was slightly taken aback at Mathias' emphasis on "all." He was obviously making sure that Webb realized Kane was part of that inclusion, though Webb doubted Mathias' veracity on the matter.

Mathias nudged Iggy and the big man slowly walked towards Webb, his face looking shyly downward all the while. When he was but a few feet from Webb, he looked back up. "Th-thank you… Webb," he stammered out, his smile never wavering. Then, unexpectedly, he gave Webb a huge hug. The strength behind the embrace made Webb's back pop, causing him to involuntarily grunt. Iggy held on for a few seconds longer before finally releasing him.

"You're welcome," Webb groaned out as he staggered to regain his footing. He didn't think he'd ever been hugged as ferociously as that.

Iggy just smiled again before ambling off to the deeper parts of the study. Mathias watched him leave before resuming their conversation.

"He can be a little much with his appreciation, but he means well."

"Glad to be appreciated," Webb groaned.

Mathias chuckled lightly. "Good night, Webb."

Webb watched him disappear before turning back towards the table and snagging another cookie to go. He took a bite and then headed out into the hallway where Uncle Mike stood waiting for him. He no longer appeared upset, but he still looked very tired from the events of the day.

"Webb," he said softly.

"Uncle Mike," Webb responded with a hug.

He returned the gesture before speaking once again. "I apologize for getting angry with you earlier. I didn't know what was going on. When Raven approached me, I was so worried that I didn't wait to get the full story out of her. I just wanted to find you and Sundown. Now, that I know what happened…"

"I understand, Uncle Mike. Besides, I don't think the Council is none too pleased with me either."

"Oh, anyone who's worth their salt here has been on the Council's naughty list at one time or another," he laughed weakly. "You did the right thing."

"Thank you, Unky. It means a lot coming from you," Webb replied earnestly. "Despite the cookies, I'm still hungry. Want to come with me to the cafeteria? I could tell you about what happened out there."

"Sorry. Not tonight, Webb," he replied wearily. "I'm really tired."

Webb nodded. "Okay then, maybe tomorrow."

Uncle Mike smiled back faintly. "You did well today, Webb. Always do good and you'll be fine here."

"I will."

His uncle nodded and then limped off down the Glorian hallways, the tap, tap, tapping of his cane ringing in Webb's ears long after he was out of sight.

— CHAPTER TWENTY-THREE —

APOLOGIES

Sundown steadily recounted to Raven what had happened—at least the parts she could remember. Badego's influence had left spotty holes in her memory. For her part, Raven kept silent as they meandered up and down the fortress hallways, letting Sundown unleash all that she had experienced and felt.

"I guess I hadn't realized my situation. No," she corrected herself almost immediately, "I didn't *want* to realize my situation and then when Webb confronted me about it yesterday, I just had to face it. But of course I couldn't do that. I had to let it eat away at me until," Sundown paused embarrassedly, "…well, you know what happened."

"And what exactly is your situation?" Raven invited.

Sundown grimaced slightly, finally replying with almost a whisper. "You know, that I'm dead. That we're all dead."

"And you really believe that?"

"Yeah," she replied candidly.

Raven suddenly grasped Sundown's arm and pinched it tightly.

Sundown jerked her arm away and began rubbing the stinging spot. "Hey! What was that for?"

"Oh! You *felt* that?" Raven asked in mock surprise.

"Yes!"

"Then I guess you're not dead after all," Raven laughed. "Sundown, your *physical* self died. The vessel that allowed you to navigate the living world died. Your soul, your essence, everything which is really you, whatever you want to call it, is still very much *alive*. True death is the removal from everything, a soulless void. You are far from dead. Otherwise, my little reminder wouldn't have hurt."

Sundown continued to rub her arm, but her composure changed dramatically. "I guess I should have listened to you more during our counseling sessions."

"Tell you a secret," Raven whispered, "I didn't heed my counselor's advice at first either."

"Who was your counselor?"

"Maybe I'll tell you about them at another time. For now, we need an understanding that from this point forward, you'll engage me, or your brother, or somebody else before things start to avalanche to the point of no return—like they almost did today."

"I promise," Sundown replied sincerely.

"You can't make it in the Dark Lands on your own, Sundown. No one can, especially not a Reclaimer. You see and remember things that all others have been spared from experiencing. It will break you if you allow it to do so."

Raven's words raced Sundown back to the moment at the veil hole. She could feel the fall, the wind cutting across her, tumbling into the emptying darkness. She pictured Webb's body being dissolved and digested inside of the horrible Whoop-Dinger. Just recalling the events was emotionally devastating. Yet to everyone but herself, these things had never happened.

"Do you understand, dear?" Raven continued.

Sundown freed herself from the haunting memories and nodded in acknowledgment.

"So, no more hiding in your room, pretending you're not there, while my knuckles grow sore knocking on your door?"

"Of course not," Sundown said, slightly surprised and embarrassed.

"Good," Raven replied. "Then enough of this wandering. I'm getting hungry. Let's get something to eat."

Despite the hour, Webb found the cafeteria still crowded with the comings and goings of his fellow Glorians. He absently wondered whether he'd ever get to know them all. He concluded that if he were in the Dark Lands for long enough, he would. For now, however, he was interested in finding only one person.

Webb swallowed and slowly walked towards the rear of the cafeteria, his mouth growing drier with each step. The hunger pangs in his stomach were now turning into pangs of apprehension. Finally, he found him eating at a table alone.

Caleb looked up silently.

"May I sit with you?" Webb asked.

"Looks like you can," Caleb said sullenly, his head nodding at the food that had suddenly materialized before Webb.

A cheeseburger, fries, and large cola. The smell was wonderful, but Caleb's frosty tone was less than inviting. Webb steeled himself and sat down.

"Caleb," Webb began, "I want to apologize."

Caleb studied him soundlessly while finishing a piece of pizza.

"I was wrong about you and I feel horrible about it," Webb continued uncomfortably.

Still, Caleb said nothing.

Webb let out a frustrated sigh. "Look, what else do you want me to say?"

Caleb swallowed his pizza and looked at Webb. "I just wanted a friend, Webb," he said solemnly. "I don't have many here and I thought you were one-"

"Caleb, I *am* your friend," Webb answered, shaking off the raw edge to Caleb's words. "That's what makes this apology that much harder! I wouldn't want anyone to accuse me the way I accused you, especially not someone I counted as a friend. I feel bad, I feel embarrassed, and I feel sorry."

Caleb's disposition appeared to change. "So what made you come to this grand realization all of a sudden?"

Webb heaved out a reluctant breath and told Caleb everything that had transpired since that morning. His telling was rather frank and unrestrained—a dry, straight-forward account reflecting his tired mood, though still several times causing Caleb's eyes to fly wide or for the occasional expletive to burst from his mouth. He especially was passionate with his outbursts during the segment where Webb revealed how Badego had whispered Caleb's memory away.

"So, Badego was playing everyone," Caleb said, astounded.

"Yes, but I think it was more the Dark Man than anything."

"And you really saw the Dark Man?"

"From a distance."

"How did you know it was him?"

"Couldn't really be anyone else," Webb shrugged.

"So you didn't get a look at who he was or what he looked like?"

"No, he was covered in a dark cloak from head to toe like some medieval druid or something. The only sense I got about him was just pure evil. No other way to describe it."

"Kind of disturbing that the Dark Man's reach extended inside Glorian."

"I think Mathias believes this is just the beginning, that things are going to get dicier."

"He said that?"

Webb shrugged again. "Not really. I'm just reading between the lines."

Caleb nodded. "Well, if the Dark Man gets in again, just remember that I'm not in league with him," he smiled.

Webb smiled back. It was an olive branch. All was not forgotten, but it was forgiven, and it was a fresh start for the two.

Both boys found their appetites again and began to eat, their conversation bouncing about sporadically for the duration of dinner. Mostly, it was Caleb bombarding Webb with curious questions about the Requiem. As they were leaving the cafeteria, they came across Raven and Sundown who were just entering.

"Webb!" Sunny called out.

"Yes?"

"I wanted to tell you that I'm really sorry I didn't believe you when you told me about Badego."

Webb smiled gently and rubbed his sister's head. "I think there have been enough apologies for the evening, Sunny. Tomorrow's a new day."

Raven nodded and regarded him kindly. "You did a brave thing, Webb." She laid her graceful hand on his shoulder in appreciation.

Webb's face flushed slightly. "Thank you," he murmured as he turned away and walked off with Caleb.

When they were out of perceived earshot, Caleb turned to Webb conspiratorially. "Man, I think she likes you," he said with a grin.

"What are you talking about?"

"Raven. I get that vibe from her."

Webb shook his head. "I wish I had your imagination. She doesn't see me as anything but a kid, just an immature kid."

"I don't know, Webb… She had *that look*."

Webb laughed. "She *always* has that *look*. Raven's just that way," he replied. "Nice dreaming though."

— CHAPTER TWENTY-FOUR —

A LOST GOODBYE

I t was a slow cozy morning the next day.

"Hello, Gustafson," Webb greeted lazily as he felt the familiar weight on his feet and heard the purring at the foot of his bed. The vocalizations of the large cat vibrated his toes, tickling them, making Webb grin. He had slept in, allowing himself a well-deserved rest.

Webb sat up and began stroking the Felidae under its soft chin. "So, you chased all of the Whoop-Dingers out of Glorian the other night?"

Gustafson's buzzing purr seemed to change to a higher tone at Webb's question, as if answering him.

Webb rolled out of bed, giving the Felidae's head one last vigorous scrub before moving to his closet. Opening the door he was struck by the realization that this morning, as with all mornings, his clothes were neatly hanging ready to be worn. Did the Dark Lands have some kind of personalized laundry service? He allowed for a slight grin at the ridiculousness of the notion before he again put on his t-shirt, jeans and letter jacket, which he was starting to establish as his "uniform," and left his room with Gustafson following close behind.

"I'm going to eat, Gus. You're welcome to tag along if you'd like." It apparently wasn't in Gustafson's plans however, as he leapt sideways up on the wall to Webb's left and sprinted away.

"Going to take a while to get used to that," Webb mumbled under his breath.

Webb altered his course from the cafeteria though its delicious smells tried to coax him into doing otherwise. Uncle Mike had been in his thoughts since they'd parted ways last night and he wanted to check in on him. He had seemed really out of it last night.

He'd never been to visit his uncle's room, but Webb had recently felt himself adapting more and more to the ways of Glorian. He was coming in tune with the place, starting to anticipate doorways, rooms and passageways before they even materialized. It was just as Mathias had promised in their early conversations—that Webb's instincts would guide him as long as he knew where he needed to go.

Webb came to a new hallway and was drawn almost trance-like to the third door on his right. He knocked on it, expecting to hear the gruff tones of his uncle or the sound of the man's cane as he shuffled to open the door. Instead, he heard another voice.

"Come in, Webb."

He twisted the knob and found that the door was unlocked. Upon opening it, he was struck with bewilderment. Mathias stood stock-still in the center of the room, but instead of being surrounded by a bed, bookshelves or the other sundry bedroom items, there was nothing, an absolute emptiness. Instead the room swirled in smoky waves of darkness. Webb looked at Mathias with marked confusion, but the older man's bleak disposition wordlessly promised him that there were no easy answers.

"…I was looking for my uncle?"

"You've come to the right place. Your instincts are being honed well." The older man smiled almost painfully; it was apparent to Webb that the gesture was a just mask to hide behind while he contemplated his next sentence.

"Where is he, Mathias?" Webb asked directly.

"Everyone has a purpose in the Dark Lands, Webb. Some purposes more subtle than others, but everyone has one. When that purpose is achieved, then their time here is over-"

"I've heard that speech before." Webb felt an ache begin to erupt within him. He didn't want to hear it. "Where is he?"

"He is gone, Webb."

"Gone? Where did he go?" Webb choked out. He blinked several times, felt his eyes become hot with welling tears.

"You know that there are four paths out of the Dark Lands. He did not die here, so he went via one of the other three paths. You should find peace in that."

"Well, *forgive me* if I don't find peace in that," Webb snapped. He looked around hastily at the undulating shadows around him before settling back on Mathias. "Which path? Which path did he take? I deserve to know *that* at least."

Mathias looked sadly upon the younger man as the emptiness continued to swirl around them. "Let's just say, he picked up where he left off," he said guardedly. "And I did not tell you that," he added.

"...Did he know that he was leaving?" Webb asked, the hurt underlying his words. "Couldn't he have said goodbye?"

"When the time draws near, one becomes exceptionally fatigued and weak. He may have recognized the signs, but could he know for certain that it was his time? No."

Webb began to turn away, but then stopped, his face now deathly pale in horrid realization. "This is my doing isn't it, Mathias?"

Mathias lowered his head and took a deep breath. "I was afraid you'd think that."

"It was one of the first things you told me!" exclaimed Webb. His voice cracked from suppressed emotion. "The Dark Lands requires a balance—a balance based on an equal number of Vindicadives and Glorians. When one Vindicadive arrives, there is a Glorian to balance it. And if a Vindicadive goes, then a Glorian must be removed as well. That's the way of things here, right?"

"I did indeed tell you there was a balance here, but I never told you that the losing of one necessitates the losing of another. That is just the machination of your grief working against you." Mathias spoke as he slowly walked out of the emptiness of the room. "Badego was a Glorian, albeit twisted by the Dark Man, but he was a Glorian still—not a Vindicadive. His casting into the Requiem had nothing to do with your uncle's fate." He placed a hand on Webb's shoulder only to have the younger man jerk away angrily.

"No… No," Webb said, his voice trailing off as he quickly left what was once his uncle's room.

Webb's footfalls thundered down the hallway. His lip began quivering, his breaths became interposed with choked sobs, but he adamantly fought to keep his composure. He wanted to go outside. *He needed to go outside.* He had to get far away from Glorian—far away from everything.

Two mammoth double doors loomed before him and Webb instinctively shot his hand forward in frustration, violently launching them outward. He walked between them, but not before one of the doors swung back to close and glanced him on the shoulder. Webb loosed a cry of equally proportioned amounts of grief, pain, and anger. He lurched around and threw his right fist hard into offending the door, resulting in a splintering pain that traveled from his now bruised and bloodied knuckles up through his wrist. He screamed again, this time staggering to his knees in anguish. He began to sob alone, his tears falling like dewdrops onto the uncaring grass. His body shook and heaved so violently that for a time, Webb thought he would not be able to take another breath.

Aside from the involuntary shaking of his shoulders, Webb sat immobile on his knees with his hands resting limply on his legs. The tears were streaming freely from his face, stinging his eyes and blurring everything before him. He could not recall ever hurting so much.

In between miserable gasps, Webb thought he heard the rumbling of a distant storm, as if his own grief had spilled over into the Dark Lands and upset the skies. It was a few moments later that he felt the first splash of rain upon his shoulder. He looked up towards the heavens and the cool tears from the darkened skies blended with his own.

The droplets began to fall harder, but Webb could not find the strength to stand and move back inside. He instead remained hunched over, continuing to cry in the rain, letting the droplets wash away the salty evidence of his grief as it kept flowing.

He didn't know how long he sat there, allowing his pain to spill from him and trickle away into the landscape. It was only when he felt a hand gently rest upon his shoulder that he awakened from his sorrowful trance.

Webb turned his head, eyes red rimmed, and saw a fuzzy blur standing behind him.

"Mathias said I would find you out here," Sundown said gently.

Webb said nothing and sniffed, wiping his eyes clear, his stiff knees feeling like they were cemented to the ground.

"I heard about Unky," she continued, her own small voice pushing back a sob.

"Yeah," was all Webb managed.

Sundown knelt beside him. "Mathias also said you were blaming yourself."

"I don't know what to believe," he muttered.

"It's not your fault."

"Oh really?" Webb shot back incredulously, turning away from her. "You're the expert now?"

Sundown grabbed his chin and forced Webb's face back in her direction. "I'm not going to let you close yourself off the way I did. I'm not letting you go down that path!"

Webb tore from his sister's grip and continued his sullen stare in the other direction, eyes boring hatefully into the ground.

"I loved Unky too, but he's gone. He is gone and you had nothing to do with it. This is bigger than you, Webb. This is bigger than all of us."

"That's twice now, Sundown. That's twice."

"What's twice?"

"He's died twice now!" Webb shouted angrily in his heartache. "Maybe this time was my fault, maybe it wasn't. But that doesn't change the fact that I won't see him again, that I'll never get to say goodbye!" Webb erupted. "If I'd been smart, I would have taken this time as a second chance to appreciate him more!"

Now, Sundown understood. This wasn't about blame—at least not all of it. This was about loss. A loss that could not be reconciled. "There are reasons…" she began to offer.

"What? What reasons?" interrupted Webb, his voice cracking again. "What was his great *purpose* here, huh? To hobble around on that cane of his?" he added dismally. The memory of his uncle limping around on his cane, the clicking noise it made haunted him, making his eyes fill again with tears.

"Haven't you figured it out? He was here to guide us, to acclimate us to the Dark Lands. Mathias and Raven did their part, but it couldn't have been done without Unky's involvement. Think about it."

"Maybe… I guess," replied Webb resentfully.

"There's no guessing to it, Webb. His role was fulfilled and now we have to take those next steps, whatever they are. It's our job to move forward. Otherwise everything that Unky did was for nothing. Everything and everyone here builds upon the other."

"Sounds like a Mathias speech," responded Webb.

"Whatever you say, Webb. But you know I'm right."

Webb didn't reply. The last raindrop landed on him as he looked out over the Dark Lands, the cool still plains, his thoughts drifting back to his first night here and all the questions he'd had. It now seemed long ago, and maybe it was, time being so circuitous in the Dark Lands. What stood out amongst the answers and non-answers was something his uncle had said. He had told Webb that not everything in the Dark Lands had an immediate reason for happening and sometimes even the reasons were not immediately satisfying, but his uncle had been insistent that in the end, *everything made sense.*

Another tear trickled down Webb's cheek. His uncle had wanted to make sure that Webb and Sundown could move along in his absence. He knew this moment might happen. Hadn't he alluded to as much in his final words? The recollection chilled him.

Webb wiped the last tear away and stood up, pulling his sister with him in the process. He then stretched out, taking in the cool, crisp air that was swimming around them.

"You understand now?" she said, noting a change in her brother.

He paused thoughtfully. "I understand that if we are going to make it here, we've got to make it together. We owe Unky that much."

"Yes we do," she smiled back.

"It's easier said than done though."

"That's why we have each other. Why we have-this place," she said, looking up at the imposing Glorian walls towering over them.

She was right. Webb smiled weakly at his sister whose hair and clothes had gotten soaked from sitting in the rain with him. It wasn't much to offer her, but that little smile was all he could muster at the moment. "Let's go inside. I'm hungry; I missed breakfast."

"And you smell like wet grass," Sundown offered with a slight smile.

"Yes, I do," Webb agreed with a laugh.

"Maybe later on tonight we could come back and watch the skies? I heard that it's beautiful at night."

"Maybe," Webb responded after a brief pause. It might be a while before he could again watch the celestial canvas in the heavens. It had been Uncle Mike who had first shown him the sight and they would always be a painful reminder for him.

Webb shook the negative feelings away and turned back to the high glimmering fortress of Glorian, wondering how long this would be their home. He opened the doors for Sundown, a distant thunder tickling his eardrums as he did so. He glanced back out over the horizon. How many more mysteries were out there? Webb strode inside and left the thoughts alone. He didn't need to worry right now. There were tomorrows and tomorrows available for such idle puzzlement. The doors shut behind them, whooshing and raking a slight breeze across their backs.

"Webb, where are we going?" Sundown asked, noticing that her brother wasn't leading them towards the cafeteria.

Webb turned around with a grin. "Just a brief detour. I want to introduce you to a friend of mine," he said, coming to a stop in front of a door.

"Who?" Sundown replied excitedly. She had always liked to meet people and make new friends.

"He's very unique," was Webb's reply as he opened the door and moved inside what appeared to Sundown as a cavernous library stacked floor to ceiling with books and papers. "I think you'll enjoy visiting him from time to time."

Sundown followed her brother in, suddenly immersed in the rich scent of fresh coffee grounds. She hurried forward eagerly with wide eyes. What a wondrous place this was.

COMING SOON

Part Two of the Dark Lands Chronology-

<u>Dark Lands: The NotWhere</u>